GARBAGE ROOM TOMB
By Michael C. Smith

SLICE OF LIFE PUBLISHING
SOLP
P.O. BOX 4028
Portsmouth, VA 23701
www.sliceoflifepublishing.com
www.solp.com

I dedicate this book to all, and everything under the watchful eye of God.
Rest in Peace, Richard "Sonny" Brown,
And all the other souls we have lost.
God willing, we will win
If not, I'm kicking ass and taking names!

AUTHOR'S NOTE:

I am somebody. Not just anybody. I am the only body who can tell you what God told me to tell you. I cannot cheat my conscious, and I damn sure refuse to censor my soul.

In the late 1980's and the early 1990's, this is what I saw and this is what I heard. This is my past and the past of many put in front of me. Many of whom, rest without peace because although their faces are gone, their stories keep repeating themselves in the lives of others in other neighborhoods, in other cities, and in other countries. Let's glimpse into the past in order to see the future, because even the future has a past.

Mike

CHAPTER ONE

TEE

At night, from a distance, all the faces and all the bodies look the same. Either someone is trying to hurt you, or they don't even notice you're alive. They don't see you searching for something or someone. They don't see that you're lost. They don't see that you are confused. Sometimes, the ones that do see you offer you things or tell you things that can only hurt you. They usually point you in the wrong direction, which is always away from where you are trying to go.

Is my moms' one of these people standing in this crowd? I wonder. As I get closer, it becomes obvious that none of them are her. I'm only fourteen, but I know it's easy to get sucked into the fun but deadly atmosphere of the so-called ghetto life, so I keep it moving.

If you don't already know, one minute people are laughing, drinking, and smoking some weed. Then, the next minute, people are getting robbed or lying dead in the street. It's the same everyday shit in the fall of 1990. What else is going on? Drugs are hitting motherfuckers hard. So hard, in fact, that they walk the streets like zombies, but these are not your regular, slow-moving zombies. These fools walk fast and for some reason have a swagger about them. They actually think they are prom kings or queens or something. In actuality, they look like they're from another planet. A spaced out, cracked out planet. They don't seem to see the cars or buses about to hit their asses. They don't seem to see the dudes in the shadows waiting for a motherfucker to slip up. These are the types that lurk in the streets with their hands on their guns.

If you have drugs, money, or gold, these are the dudes who get you when you least expected it. The streets are always watching, hunting for meat, bones, or crumbs. This is how the game is played.

Some get high; some get money, and some get over. Then, there are the ones that sink deeper and deeper into it all.

My moms is on that crack shit too. That's why I'm out here looking for her. Mrs. Mona Jackson is her name. She was beautiful back in the day. That was until my pops got her hooked on crack. He overdosed when I was eight years old.

Even after my pops died, my moms didn't stop. She still be walking around here like she's hot shit, shaking her ass. The little bit of ass she has left, anyway. She'd be straight cracked out, and even worse, she is still wearing the same shit from '84.

My mom's swagger is downright nasty, but she still tries to walk like a supermodel. It would be funny if it wasn't so damn pitiful to see. She wears her clothes like she wears her life. She just doesn't give a fuck.

I don't know how many times I have watched her small frame, draped in outdated clothes, emerge from a rundown building. In my hood, the wannabe thugs hustle out of the many rundown buildings and drug spots, if their money isn't fucked up from doing drugs themselves or if they haven't spent their re-up money on bitches, clothes, and jewelry. You know, stupid shit like that. Speaking of which, I could use a gold chain right now.

"Yo, Ma! Ma!" I yell from across the street, while running towards her. She needs to bring her ass home.

"Ma! Oh—You ain't my moms, but— Damn! — You look like her. I'm sorry, miss."

"You damn right! I ain't your momma! My kids are at home 'sleep, where your ass should be instead of out here in these streets."

When I get closer to her face, it's more fucked up and fake looking than my mother's. Even worse, this bitch has the nerve to have on bright red lipstick.

"My bad, bitch!"

I walk away from the lady fast because she looks like she would have fight her own shadow.

I have already spent more time looking for Mona's ass than I usually do. Usually, it only takes half an hour to an hour tops to find her, but, this time, I've been searching for her for way over an hour. Wherever she was, she don't want to be found. That's for damn sure. I head back home, fed up with all the bullshit. Plus, tomorrow is a school day.

I don't have cable television. Instead, I have seven channels on my TV—2, 4, 5, 7, 9, 11 and 13. My TV has rabbit ears sticking out the top, and you better believe one antenna is broke off. We replaced that with a coat hanger a long time ago. Video games? Forget about it! If you don't have Atari or Genesis, you don't have shit. There is really only two other things for a kid to look forward to— school and the summer time. Both guarantee your stomach will be full. Shit! Some of the best food I eat is in school or in the summer programs. You know the ones I'm talking about— the programs where they give out free breakfast and lunch. Oh, I know you know. Anyways, once I get back on the block, guess who's coming out of my building? Yeah. Mona Jackson, herself.

"Where the fuck was you at?" Mona yells.

"I was looking for you," I answer, but what I really want to say is, "Where the fuck was you at?"

I just stand there, staring down at the concrete. I try to avoid looking at her directly. My mother is definitely high, and seeing her like this always hurt me, but it's more than that. My mother scares me, and it's not just the beatings that make me afraid of her. It's also the animal-like facial expressions she makes while she beats the shit out of me.

She grabs my shirt tightly and says, "Well, take your ass upstairs! I'll be up in a minute."

Before I can think of something that would persuade her to come upstairs, she is already doing the fast zombie walk that I was telling you about before.

"But, Ma, ain't nothing upstairs to eat!" I yell.

"I seen some hot dogs in the fridge. Now, get your ass upstairs, Tee. You got school tomorrow."

My mother quickly distances herself from me, mumbling every step of the way. As her voice fades, her image shrinks.

"You ain't got no business being out here anyway. And why you always worried about ..."

Before I knew it, she had flown up the block, and the bitch don't even have wings.

Once upstairs, I fix myself some franks and beans. I watch TV and waited for Mona to bring her ass home.

Several hours later, I wake up to the sound of static blazing on the TV screen. I don't know what time it is, so I decide to go back to sleep, but before I can close my eyes, I hear Mona saying, "Tee! Tee! I'm not going to tell you again to get your ass up, and you better not be late for school."

"Alright! Alright! I'm up," I yell back as she leaves my room and goes back into her bedroom.

I turn to the wall in an attempt to get away from the shrill voice that keeps invading my much needed sleep and try to get back to the memories of last night's dream. It's still fresh in my head. I want to get back to where the dream left off. *Let's see. I was on a beach with a ...*

"Tee! Didn't I tell you to get the fuck up?"

I jump out of bed this time because the sound of her voice is like nails on a chalkboard.

On the way to the bathroom, I kick my cat Deuce. He always trips me by sticking his head and body in between my legs as I walk past him. This is love at its best, people. He shows me love by harassing me.

Really, he just wants to eat. I show love by, first, taking my morning piss. Next, I feed his ass and give him fresh water out of the bathroom sink. Then, I ask him a question.

"How come you get to eat before me?"

"Meow."

I guess he know more about love than I do.

After making a ham and cheese sandwich for breakfast, I go back into the bathroom to wash up and get dressed. Now, my school isn't far, but, for some reason I'm always late. For a hot minute, I consider taking my book bag, but nah...*How can I be cool lugging around a book bag all day?* All I have to do is just ask somebody for a pen and a piece of paper in class. I head for the door after snatching the two dollars Mona left for me on the table. *Did I get everything?* I wonder while I walk back to the kitchen to get something to drink. Once I open the refrigerator, I see that the Kool-Aid is gone. The pitcher is empty except for a couple of ice cubes and a few drops of water from the melted ice. I decide not to drink the nasty water in the pitcher because our refrigerator makes the water taste stale. At the same time, if you take a spoon and scraped the ice from inside the freezer, you will never need to drink water again. Freezer ice is better than sex. After scraping the ice shavings from out the freezer six or seven times, I head for the front door. This time, for real.

Once the door shuts, I remember to check for my key.

"I don't believe this shit. I ain't got my key."

I did tell you I was always late for school. I go back into the apartment and search for twenty minutes for a key that's been in my top shirt pocket the whole time. It's like a ghost be messing with me sometimes, moving shit and then putting it back, like it's a practical joke or something.

I know I have to hurry up, so I can't wait for the elevator. The way shit breaks down in my building, it probably ain't working anyway. I have no problem taking the stairs, and besides, it's a lot faster.

I check the door to my apartment to make sure it's locked before running past the elevator and to the staircase door. Like so many mornings before, I jump down the stairs with one hand on the banister. The banister helps me to control my jump and makes it possible to clear all ten steps before the staircase door even closes. I have practiced jumping down these stairs for years and, if you've ever been chased down a flight of stairs, then you know what I'm talking about. I live all the way on the eighth floor, so I got a long way to go before I reach the first floor lobby.

After my first jump, I make the turn on the stairwell and jump down the next ten steps to get to the seventh floor. I jump and turn again to get to the sixth floor. I repeat this on the fifth floor and again on the fourth, but, before my feet land to make the turn, while coming up the stairs in between the third and fourth floor, I land in front of a full grown pit bull. Our eyes lock as surprise overcomes us both. The brownish-red pit bull jumps back as if running is its first option. Then, the dog's facial expression changes from surprise to anger. It growls at me like I stole its bone or something. It must realize it has no reason to fear me, or it must be picking up the smell of fear I'm wearing like a jacket. I hadn't stolen its bone; I am the bone. The pit bull is the hunter, and I am the prey. This mother fucker's got me, and we both know it.

"Oh, shit!" are the only words that come out of my mouth. My legs want to move, but they don't. The same thought keeps racing through my mind and playing over and over in my head. It echoes a million times every millionth of a second. *I'm dead! I'm dead!*

The dog lunges for my throat, so I put up my hands to stop him. I now know it's a male because his lunge revealed his underside and his balls. His neck is wide, and his teeth seem to grow in midair. The pit's mouth is wide open and just inches from his target— my neck. *I'm dead! I'm dead!*

At the same time, his front paws are up in the air. He's determined to smash his muscular body into my small teenage frame. The collision knocks both of us down. The pit bull lands on top of me. The back of my head slams into the floor. I feel a brutal ringing sensation. It goes from my head to my toes. Something tells me to put my left arm up and jam it into the mouth of the pit as it began to rip and shake my arm like a rag doll. In the meantime, his eyes remain locked on my eyes. He's focused on my neck for the killer blow. My head is ringing like a bell but I am still able to instinctively put my right arm out as he releases my mangled left arm and goes for my neck again. This time, flesh rips from my arm, as the pit bull falls backwards. He takes a piece of me before making a complete 360° turn. He then repositions himself for another attack. I jump up from the cold and now bloody floor and begin to run and crawl up the stairs. I get to the fourth floor staircase door, but I only make it up eight steps before the pit bites down hard on my ankle. I scream like a bitch as he pulls me back down to the fifth step. I grab onto the banister in the hopes of maintaining some of the progress I have just gained, but, just when you think you're moving up, they truly drag you back down. So here we are, me face down, holding on to the banister, and the dog locked on to my ankle, pulling and tugging. I know I can only hold on for a few more seconds, and the fucking pain is unbearable. A wave of dizziness rushes over me, and I think I went to sleep for a second. My vision is blurry, but I can see blood everywhere. The sight of my very own blood makes me want to throw up.

Finally, my hand slips and I let go of the banister. The dog then drags me back to the middle of the third and fourth floor stairwell. This is the same spot where the attack had first taken place. I roll over, and the staircase seems to roll over too. Everything is spinning, and I begin to vomit up the sandwich I had just eaten for breakfast. I can even taste the franks and beans I had eaten last night. The smell of vomit and blood in the air must have confused the dog because it lets go of my ankle. If just for a moment, the dog has to taste the irresistible mixture of food that I vomited up. I take the opportunity to crawl backwards up the stairs. Slowly at first, but then with every drop of energy I have, I sprint up the few remaining steps. I finally make it to the fourth floor staircase door. I fling open the door and run through the hallway of the fourth floor. I keep running, too. I don't stop to look back, and I don't stop to bang on anybody's apartment door. I run straight to the garbage room, which every floor in my building has. I go into the garbage room and slam the door shut behind me.

Darkness. That is all I see. Somebody is always stealing the light bulb out of the garbage rooms. Even if there was a light bulb, it wouldn't make no difference. the light goes out when the door is closed. *Cheap-ass bastards always trying to save money. Thank God I can see just a little light bit of light from under the door.*

The garbage room is the size of a very, very small closet, and I'm sitting on top of some nasty trash bags. All the trash that doesn't fit in the small chute on the wall is just thrown on the floor. The kids on the fourth floor be doing that shit when their parents tell them to take out the garbage. I do the same thing up on the eighth floor when it's time for me to dump the garbage. I just toss that shit on the floor. *What's that smell?* I wonder. It smells like shit in here. Damn! It is shit in here from some damn baby's Pampers. The smell clashes with the rotten food, my blood, and my vomit.

I want to leave, but I'm too scared to move. *Maybe, if I crack open the door just a little bit I can at least, be free from the darkness,* I try to rationalize, but once again, my body refuses to move. I am just gonna have to sit here until I hear somebody walk past the garbage room, and so I sit and sit and sit. It seems like hours have passed but I don't have a watch. Still, nobody walks past the garbage room.

Sometimes, I hear people on the upper floors dumping their trash, or is it the lower floors? It's hard to tell. I can hear garbage chute doors slamming and garbage traveling behind the walls as it makes its way down to the basement.

"Help! Help me, somebody! Please! Help me!" I yell as my voice gets weaker by the minute.

Nobody comes to help me. I hear the sounds of mice and rats, moving around in the garbage room with me. When they get quiet, I hear the sounds of the roaches and water bugs moving around in the room with me. Some of the movements are heavy, and some of the movements are light, but there is definitely more than one thing in this room with me.

So, here my mangled body remains, just like the nasty garbage. The pit bull broke more than my body. It has also, broken my soul.

The light from under the door is starting to fade, and so am I. My eyelids slowly shut into darkness, total darkness.

CHAPTER TWO

THE CREW

OHME

"Yo! Who's gonna get the beer and Dutch Masters?"

I'm not talking to nobody in particular; I'm just asking whose turn is it to go to the store. I don't have a name, but you can call me Ohme. I'm so real that whoever is telling my story better not fuck it up. I'm the dude sitting over here on this old, dusty couch. No, not him, that one's me right there. I'm the one sitting on the couch with the roaches crawling up the arm rest. Yeah. That's me.

As soon as I ask the question about the store, this clown motherfucker, sitting at the dining room table all the way on the other side of the room, mind you, yells out, "Fuck them Dutchies! Bring back some Phillies!"

That's the Destroyer who just yelled that shit out. We call him Des for short because, if you are having a good day, clown boy over there knows how to destroy it quick. He's a straight fuck up. I'm not going to waste my breath responding to that shit. That's X's homeboy anyway. I say X because names aren't important in my business. I sit quietly, looking at Des the Clown, and I'm staring at him hard too. I look at him so hard that I can almost see right through him. Lucky for him, too, 'cause if I see right through him, I will pull out and shoot him. I pluck a roach off the armrest of the couch, just like I am about to do to this fool. Just then, Captain Cool comes out the bathroom.

"I was just about to go to the store," said X.

Small disagreements get big fast up in this crib. I know it, and my partner in crime, X, right there knows it, too.

I used to hustle for X's pops back in the day. I was about seventeen, eighteen at the time.

Let's just say X's pops name is Biggs. He's big time and no joke. He is the type of dude that buys toys for kids in the neighborhood when it aint even Christmas. You wouldn't believe how much money he was getting out in these streets. Biggs looked out for anybody that showed him respect, and, trust me, he deserved all the respect he got. The only problem I had with Biggs was that he was too real. He could be cold as ice when he wanted to be. For example, when X ran away from home at sixteen years old, Biggs threw a good-bye party.

Hold up! Look at punk-ass Des, sitting over there. He don't know how close he is to getting it. Now, Des had been a real momma's boy when we were kids. His moms didn't let him go outside; she wouldn't let him have any friends. Yo, she wouldn't fucking let him do nothing. I think she had abandonment issues because of Des's pops or maybe her own pops. I really don't know. What I do know is all that changed when his moms got hooked on every drug that was out in the 80s. After that, she didn't even want his ass in the house with her. How do I know? I told you that I used to hustle for Biggs when I was a kid. When Des was forced to come outside, he wasn't prepared or equipped to survive one step outside his door. Basically, he got fucked up every day. Don't look at me. I never bothered the kid. I was too cool for that. I was probably the only kid on the block that was in school, had a part time job, and still found time to hustle for Biggs.

Both of my parents worked, but when we did end up at home together, we barely spoke to one another. I was the black sheep of the family. It was Biggs who schooled me about life and these streets. Yeah, I know, I had it going on. But, still, something wasn't right. I felt like the world was taking advantage of my hard work. I got good grades in school. I busted my ass on the job, and I could sell anything to anybody. I wanted more, and I wanted to be the best at something. I needed to find what it was I was good at and conquer it. Make something. Change its name to my name and own it. Let the world know I owned that shit, if even for just a minute, like what Michael Jordan did to basketball. No! Fuck that. I wanted to be the person who invented basketball. I wondered, *If slavery is dead, then why are there so many rich slaves out here?* I see rich slaves on TV all the time. When their bosses tell them to sit down, they sit down. When their bosses tell them to eat, they eat. Where is the freedom in that?

I always thought like this, but I had been worse before the streets doused the flame that burns in my soul, the flame that dreams are made or played of.

Now, every thug up in Apartment 4B had a story to tell, but it's not my business to tell it.

"Yo, X! When you go to the store, can you please bring me back some Dutchies?"

X looks at me and nods, so I know I'm good.

"Yeah. Yeah. Let me get some Phillies, not them Dutch Master shits, a box of Newports, and two forty ounces. Get me two cold ones out the back of the freezer," Des orders.

I did tell you this fool had issues with his mother, didn't I? This time, when I stare at him, he tried to play gangsta 'cause X is around. This motherfucker is actually trying to look right through me. *Yeah...tonight, he dies*, as I contemplate the when, where and how.

"Anybody else want something from the store?" X yells.

People come out of every room to tell X what they want from the store. They come out of the two bedrooms, and they come from the kitchen. My little man Tuff emerges from out of the closet. You would have never known he was in there if it wasn't for the phone wire that stretched from the kitchen wall into the closet. I'm not talking about one of them high tech phones. I'm talking about the phone where you put your finger through the holes to dial your number.

4B is X's crib, but you wouldn't know it. It had become the neighborhood spot ever since X had run away some fourteen years ago. If you was a criminal on my block, you had lived in 4B at one time or another.

"Let every character play their part," X would say. Speaking of X, I can tell my partner in crime don't want to go to the store, and I sense a whole lot of frustration over there, waiting for that pen and paper. Everybody plays their part, huh?

X finally heads for the door with the list, but stops short and yells out, "Yo! Somebody got to come with me and help carry this shit!"

There are no volunteers. This time no one comes out of the back rooms. No one comes from the kitchen. Nobody gets up from the dining room table, and my man Tuff stays in the closet, talking on the phone.

"Fuck everybody! I'm going to the store for me, and that's it," X yells out. Before I can get up and go, the arguing starts, and it ends with Little Ed going to the store with X.

"I don't believe this shit! Y'all some lazy motherfuckers! Everybody wants something, but nobody wants to go get it."

"I'm coming, X," Little Ed volunteers.

I get the feeling that he doesn't want to go to the store either.

 It's usually the youngest, the weakest, or the poorest that ends up going to the store. In X's case, it's the shepherd tending to the sheep.

X and Little Ed walk out the door. I grab my sawed off shotgun that has been keeping me company on the couch and stand up. I walked towards Des, but it's only at the last second that I turn from him and go to lock the front door. Before can I lock it, Little Ed pushes the door open and walks back into the apartment, smiling.

"X said to tell y'all motherfuckers to cough up some dough if you want something from the store. If you don't put any money in, you don't put your hands in."

As Little Ed goes around the apartment collecting money, he writes down who gave what and how much they gave him. I gave him a hundred dollar bill just off of GP. He grabs the trash bag out the kitchen and heads out the door again. I lock the door and go back to my spot on the couch. Me and my company.

CHAPTER THREE

THE DISCOVERY

X

"X, you ain't gonna believe this."

"I already know, Ed. Some motherfuckers didn't get shit. Just pass me the trash bag, so I can dump it, while you go ring for the elevator."

So, I go to the garbage room to dump the trash. Something tells me that, if I didn't do it, nobody would. Every character plays their...

Oh, my bad! We weren't properly introduced. I'm the infamous X. Even if I don't know you, chances are I still know you. You're as special as a snowflake. Meditate on that for a while.

"Yo! What the fuck?"

"What's wrong?" Ed yells out from where he stands at the elevator door.

He hesitates at first, but finally he walks over to the garbage room doorway where I am standing.

"Oh, my God!" he says as he looks down into the garbage room. The body is curled up in the corner on top of some trash bags. There are roaches and mice running for cover, but the large water bugs continue to drink whatever blood that has pooled or smeared on the wall. They seem unfazed by our presence.

"I think that's that crack head lady's kid. You know the one up on the eighth floor?" he said.

I wasn't sure, so I step into the filthy garbage room to get a closer look. Only then do the water bugs run for cover.

"I don't know, Ed. You sure?"

"Yeah, I'm sure. We went to the same school before I got kicked out."

I search for a place on the kid's body that isn't covered with blood, but I can't find no such place. The poor kid's head slides down the wall and onto the filthy trash bags. Ed immediately lets the garbage room door go and helps me secure the kid's head. With no other place to grab, I go for shorty's belt and slide the lifeless body as carefully as possible off the garbage bags , out of the garbage room, and into the hallway.

"Yo, Ed! Call the fucking ambulance and hurry up!"

Shorty stays in my arms until the ambulance people haul the body away on a stretcher.

CHAPTER FOUR

MANGLED

X

It's been almost two weeks since the paramedics had run up the stairs to get Tee's mangled body from the fourth floor hallway. Because the elevator was broken, they had to use the stairs. One of the paramedics told me that they were stopped dead in their tracks by an awful surprise on the third floor staircase. A beast was hovering over a smaller animal, taunting it with small bites to its flesh, nudging it to move. He said they went back down the stairs slowly, as he

fought back the urge to puke in response to what he'd seen. It took, at least, twenty minutes for the cops to arrive, plus another five minutes before they could piece together what the EMS workers were trying to tell them. It had to have been a hell of a sight.

When I saw the cop describe the scene on the eleven o'clock news, I also saw the horror in his eyes. He described hearing ungodly sounds from an animal on the stairs. When all was said and done, a huge pit bull laid dead in the staircase. More importantly, a young kid was dead on the scene. He had been mauled by that pit bull.

Tee survived, if you were wondering. They say what doesn't kill you only makes you stronger. But, in reality, it just makes your outside shell tougher. While on the inside, you're scared as shit that it could happen to you again. You lose your sense of security.

Me and Little Ed went to the hospital every day until it was time for Tee to come home, and afterwards, Little Tee quickly became a part of the 4B Crew.

I had a long conversation with shorty's moms, Mona. Nothing fancy.

Just something about her owing my soldiers four hundred dollars worth of credit, how we killed motherfuckers for less than that and making sure shit like the dog attacking Tee doesn't happen again. I told Mona that Tee was special and that I was gonna look out for the kid from now on.

Damn! I wish I could have saved that other kid in the staircase. On the day of shorty's funeral, me and the crew were in the lobby of our building, drinking and smoking, just doing anything to take our minds off that little eight-year-old. I guess you could say it was a ghetto farewell party.

Des was cracking jokes about the kid, but, mostly, he was joking on Tee, saying shit like,

"What do you feed a pit bull if you ain't got no food?"

"What?" somebody in the crowd replied.

"A Tee-bone steak," Des answered.

Some people laughed, and some people didn't. I looked over at Tee, who was wearing a phony smirk, but I could tell the memories of the whole situation burned deep.

"Okay, everybody! Listen up! I got an announcement to make,"

I stand up on some bricks that hold some fake plants. These are the only decorations in our rundown lobby. We use the bricks as chairs and tables to rest the boxes of pizza, cups of liquor, and forty ounces bottles on.

"We opening a new spot. I got us a new crib on the third floor. Right underneath the one we got now. It's going to be me, Ohme, Little Ed, and Little Tee moving into the new apartment, while Des, Tuff, Shy, and the rest of y'all are going to hold down the crib in 4B."

"My mom's ain't going for that shit," Tee interrupts, while looking at me with a whole lot of disappointment.

"I already spoke to Mona, shorty, and it's cool, as long as your ass stays out of trouble and away from dogs. You scared the shit out of us, Tee."

This is how I let Tee know that not everybody is cold-hearted like Des.

"One more thing, y'all. Nobody, I mean nobody, better come down stairs to 3B for nothing. If you need something, call Ed, and he'll bring it to you."

"Hold up, X. Y'all ain't leaving me upstairs with these savages," said Tuff, making sure to add some humor to his statement, but I still don't like being interrupted, and I can tell he's not joking.

"Just get with Ohme, Tuff. He'll figure something out."

Ohme and Tuff step to the side to work out a business arrangement.

"Now, what was I saying? Oh, yeah! Don't fucking come downstairs for nothing. Des, if anybody disrespects what I'm saying, just do what Biggs would do."

Des could see the seriousness on my face when I brought up my pops. Anyone else would have been scared, but all my words do is excite Des to the point that he hollers out, "Now, that's what I'm talkin' 'bout!"

I nonchalantly go back to eating my pizza, and that is that.

"Now, back to your ass," Des turns and looks directly at Tee. "Where did they find you at? Oh, shit! Oh, shit! That's right. I almost forgot. They found your ass like a mummy in a tomb, a garbage room tomb. Oh, shit! That rhymes. That's what I'ma call you from now on. Your name ain't Tee no more. Now, it's Garbage Room Tomb!"

Some people laugh, and some don't think the shit is funny.

"Des, you can't call shorty Garbage Room Tomb. That shit is too damn long," Little Ed steps out and sticks up for Little Tee.

Now, Des always has a quick response for little pricks that try to ruin his jokes. I didn't say it, Des did, and that's was exactly what he calls Little Ed.

"Hold up, you little prick. Who you calling 'shorty'? You and Garbage Room Tomb are the same size and almost the same age. Sit your little ass down and eat some pizza."

It's a losing battle arguing with Des, so Little Ed steps back into the mix of the crew.

"All right. Garbage Room Tomb's too long for you? I'll shorten it up a little. Tee's new name is GT, short for Garbage Room Tomb or Garbage Tee."

GT tries hard to ignore Des by grabbing a slice of pizza and sticking close to me for the rest of the day, but that's not gonna cut it. Everybody has to play their part.

CHAPTER FIVE

GT

TEE

It hadn't been that long ago since I was attacked by the pit bull. I'm glad to be alive but sad somebody had to die. The doctor said that I'm still suffering from "some psychological stress caused by my traumatic experience". He claims that this is what's keeping me from wanting to go back to the school. Bullshit! I won't be going back to school because it used to be fun, but now, I don't see nothing funny about it.

Today is the day I move into the new crib in 3B. My bags are packed, and I'm ready to go. Besides my moms, I don't have any real family or friends. When you think about it, who does? The people you call your family don't really know you, and you don't really know them. The same could be said about your friends. Where will life take them? What will they become? You don't know. All you know is, that's your friend, and that's your family. Now, what if they don't know themselves?

I still can't believe my moms is letting me move in with my crew. She probably sold me for an eight ball. X, Ohme, and Little Ed are more than just friends. Now, they're like the family I had never had but always wanted. I don't even know the last time I had seen my moms. She's been acting strange lately, even for her. I knocked on her bedroom door one day to see if she was alright, and she had the nerve to tell me to "stop knocking on my door, I'm sleep." How was she "sleep" when she was talking to me through the door?

My crew comes upstairs to get me, and no one seems more excited than Ed.

"You ready? You still coming?" he asks, while smiling like the Kool-aid kid.

"Yeah, I'm ready, but I need help with my bags," I tell him.

All eyes look down at my feet where everything I own is packed and ready to go. They see all my stuff and bust out laughing.

"What's so funny?" I ask.

Ohme shakes his head in disbelief, "You don't need that, that, or that."

He points at everything I own, except my suitcase full of dirty clothes. They help me put everything else back in my room. All my prize possessions. *Maybe I should keep my ass here with my mother,* I wonder.

When we get to the door of the new apartment, X gives me a key and motions for me to open the door. I fumble with the key for a few seconds before finally opening the door.

"Oh, my God" is all I can say.

The first thing I notice is the brand new white carpet that seems to travel throughout the entire apartment. I walk further inside and see a huge black leather couch with a matching loveseat swallowing the entire left wall of the living room. On the opposite wall is a black entertainment center with a huge TV sitting in it. There's a stereo system with speakers that stand taller than me and Ed. I kid you not. The black curtains over the two windows hang all the way down to the floor, and in front of each window are statues of lions. It kinda reminds me of those statues you see in books and shit, except these have fake plants flowing down their heads where their manes should have been. On the walls are paintings of animals, birds, and even insects. There's a huge glass dining room table to the left of the living room, and the dining room chairs look like they got stolen from a castle somewhere.

The kitchen is the next room I go into. I notice it's situated just like the kitchen on the fourth and eighth floor. Surprisingly though, these wooden cabinets look brand new. The ones I'm used to seeing look like they have been painted over a hundred times. I fling open the cabinets, and my Kool-Aid smile tells it all. We got food, real food! I walk over to the refrigerator, and there's no disappointment there either. The fridge is packed with food. It looked like one of the refrigerators from a TV show. Of course, the TV shows never have the cases of beer and liquor chilling inside the fridge, ya know!

I step out the kitchen, so I can peep the bathroom. Once I cut the light on, there is no mistaking the zebra striped shower curtains that hypnotize me when I stare at them too long. All the rugs in the bathroom are black and fluffy, even the toilet bowl cover is black and fluffy. We even had zebra striped towels and wash cloths in this motherfucker.

When I finally get to the bedroom, Ed is already claiming the bed next to the window. I don't really care because it's not like I'm up on the eighth floor. Up there, the prettiest thing to look at is the sky. The closet door is open, and I look at Ed for a minute in disbelief. Then, we both start laughing.

"That's mine?"

"Yeah, buddy!" Ed replies.

"Yours is on the left, and mine is on the right."

The closet is full of new clothes with the tags still on them. On my side of the closet floor are two sneaker boxes. I try them on immediately.

"Tee, check this out," Ed calls to me from across the room. I take my eyes off my new Jordans long enough to look up at him. He's holding a controller for the new Sega Genesis.

"Oh, shit!"

He's playing *Mike Tyson's Punch Out!* I make a mental note to check it out later when he's not around. This way, I can practice my skills and show him who the master is later on.

Next, I go to check out the rest of the apartment. I peek into X's room where everything is pretty much hooked up the same way as me and Ed's room. I can't help but notice that everything, I mean everything, is either black or white, give or take the green plants and fake trees that are spread around here and there.

Ohme has the living room all to himself. There's something about a couch and a TV that gives Ohme some peace, or it might be the fact that Des's ass is upstairs, Ohme doesn't have to hear all that bullshit Des is famous for. I'm loving it too, because I really hate that Garbage Room Tomb bullshit.

Later on, Ohme cooks us a big dinner. We sit at the dining room table to eat, which is a first for me. After dinner, X and Ohme smoke trees, while Ed takes a whole bottle of Hennessey to the head. I don't do none of that shit, not yet anyway. Seeing my moms fucked up all the time makes me want to fight that shit for as long as possible, unless the streets get to me and made me fold like a bitch, but I have to do something. The sugar rush from a big piece of chocolate cake will have to do.

I sit at the table, feeling good and real relaxed. The conversation starts with small talk. Then, it grows into a discussion about dudes, chicks, and money. You know, life in general. A lot of talk, nothing specific and certainly nothing personal. Eventually, the topic of God comes up. Before the night is over, I find out that I'm not the only one going through some shit. I really feel Ed's pain when he says, "My parents were Jehovah's Witnesses and got killed in a car accident." Ed stops talking just long enough to put the bottle of liquor up to his mouth. He swallows two big gulps before speaking again.

"After that, I went to live with my grandmother. She was my heart and the only person in the world that loved me, even when my parents were alive. I came home from school one day and found her at the kitchen table 'sleep, except she wasn't 'sleep."

He takes twice as many swallows before continuing.

"After I lost my grandmother, they put me in a foster home with the sickest foster parents they could find me. These perverted motherfuckers thought I was there to satisfy their twisted sexual needs. Not long after that, I ran away and lived on the streets for a while. One night, I was standing outside the corner store asking for change, and that's where I met X."

The more liquor Ed drinks, the more he talks. The more he talks, the weaker he becomes.

X and Ohme, on the other hand, seem stronger as the night moves on. How can two totally different people get along so well? X is some type of Christian renegade, while Ohme comes off as a quiet, thugged out Muslim.

One starts a sentence, and the other one finishes it. I can tell they've been cool for a long time. I feel a little left out because my moms was never big on religion, and I don't really know that much about God. Still, the vibe is right, and they give me a crash course on the Great One. I can feel the love in the room, so much so, that it sends chills up my spine.

CHAPTER SIX

ANYTHING FOR TWO HUNDRED DOLLARS

TEE

The sound of the phone ringing at five sharp the next morning interrupts my sleep, but it is the sound of X screaming for Ed to "Get the fuck up" that wakes me up completely.

Ed grabs a book bag from under his bed and leaves the apartment. He looks like he is sleepwalking. This motherfucker doesn't take a bath; change his clothes, or nothing. I shake my head and go back to sleep. I'm awakened again by the smell of something cooking. Ed must have come back while I was asleep because when I got up, he's passed out on his bed.

X is in the kitchen cooking up turkey bacon, eggs, and cheese, while Ohme is in the living room rolling up a fat Bob Marley spliff. It feels weird not having Deuce crying and rubbing his big head against my legs. I take my morning piss, shower, brush my teeth and get dressed. Me, X, and Ohme eat breakfast as we joke on Ed's drunk ass. Last night he had spilled some liquor on the new white carpet.

"That motherfucker's going to scrub that stain out when he gets his ass up," says Ohme.

As I get up to leave, X looks up from a plate of half-eaten food, "Yo, Tee! You can do whatever you want while you living here, but you have to stay out of trouble, and don't ever tell nobody where you live at."

X pulls out two hundred dollars and a library card, and then slides them across the table to me.

"We can't have you going stupid up in here, especially since your ass don't go to school no more. Go read a book."

I take the money and library card but hesitate for a second.

"What am I supposed to do with all this money?"

Before X can answer me, Ohme jumps into the conversation.

"Do whatever you want with it, but the more money you save, the more shit you can get."

I pretend to know what the fuck Ohme is talking about.

"All right! All right! I got you. First, I'ma go see my moms and give her some of this loot. Then, I'ma head over to the library and get five books, nah, ten books. Anybody want something from the store? I'm buying."

I feel like a big baller with two hundred dollars in my hand. This is the most money I ever had in my life.

"Yeah! Bring me back some salt and vinegar potato chips and a Pepsi, but Tee, I need you to do me a favor before you come back."

"Whatever you need, X."

I realize at this moment, that I would do anything for two hundred dollars.

"I need you to go upstairs to 4B and get Ed's book bag."

"That's nothing. Is that's all you need me to do?"

"Yeah! That's all, but bring it straight here, Tee. Don't bullshit around, and don't let nobody take that shit from you."

X looks me dead in the eyes, so I know this picking up a book bag is some serious shit.

"Don't never let nobody take nothing from you. NOTHING!" Ohme said, quickly throwing rule number one at me.

"I got you," I said, while hurrying out the door. I'm afraid that Ohme will realize, once again, that I have no idea what the fuck he is talking about.

Once I get outside the apartment and into the hallway, my eyes go from watching the elevator door, to watching the staircase door. I take it all in as the fear builds up inside of me, but, just as quickly as my eyes consider it, my brain makes me push the elevator button instead, 'cause, if you think I'm taking the motherfucking stairs, you crazy.

After the elevator takes its sweet time to come, I get on it and ride it up to the eighth floor. I can't count the number of times I have gotten off the elevator, but, this time, something feels different. Life feels good, but, more importantly, I can't wait to give my moms some of this two hundred dollars. I feel rich, but it don't mean shit if I can't share it with my moms. Damn! I love her, even if she is a crack head. I walk to my old apartment door with a cool swagger, like I just won the lottery or something. I use my old key to open the door.

"Yo, Ma! Ma! Yo, Mommy!"

I search every room, looking for her, but she isn't home. Deuce the cat is gone, too. Moms must have finally got rid of his stupid ass. *Fuck it!* I thought, *I'll just come back later*. As I made my way to the door, I notice a beat up envelope sitting in between the salt and pepper shakers that have been sitting empty on the small kitchen table for as long as I can remember. I go for the envelope 'cause it just feels like it's been waiting there for me.

"Oh, shit! It's my pops' gold medallion."

His gold butterfly medallion is decked out with cubic zirconium. A lot of the stones are missing, but holding his butterfly brings back memories. My pops used to rock this medallion on a crazy fat chain. Pops was the man.

"I thought Moms said he had sold all his jewelry to get high."

My hands start shaking as I reach back into the envelope. I'm afraid to read the note that's c with the medallion but, also, afraid not to read it.

*****

Hey, baby!

There is so much I want to say, but I don't know how to say it. I'm stuck on words. I mean the words are here, but I just don't have the heart or soul to let them out. I lost my heart and soul a long time ago. Maybe it was when I lost my mother, or maybe it was because I didn't know my father. Maybe it was when I lost the only man I ever loved— your father. I've lost family and friends. I've lost everything and everyone. So, yeah! I smoke crack. You better never fuck with that shit, either. When I seen you in the hospital with all those tubes hooked up to you, I knew for damn sure I'd lost you— my last reason for living. I begged God to save your little ass. I had never prayed so hard in my life and probably will never pray that hard again. The crazy shit about it is, when I left the hospital and got back to our building, X and some kid named Red or Ed was getting off the elevator when I was getting on. I knew X's father from back in the day. Anyway, Fred said they were the ones who pulled you out the garbage room and saved your life. He said they were just about to go see you in the hospital. I thanked them both, but X said I should thank God because something told them "to dump the garbage that day". If it wasn't for that voice, they would have never found you in time.

X gave me some money. That's how I got your father's medallion out the pawn shop, again. Every time me and your daddy needed some money to get high, we would pawn something. We lost a lot of shit that way but not the butterfly. I always found a way to get it back. There's something about it. It's special to me, like you. Even X said there's something special about you, so special that they're going to make sure nothing else ever happens to you.

I really can't tell you what else they said to me that day because I got so fucked up that night, fucked up to the point that I woke up in the same hospital as you. I had almost overdosed like your daddy. The doctor asked me if I knew that crack kills. I told him, "Yeah. Tell me something I don't know," so he said that I've been sick for a long time and that the cancer is going to kill me before the crack does. Tee, I ain't got much longer. I wish I could have did things differently, did more for

*you and been there more for you. I remember, a
long time ago, I used to be a store manager. I
used to take you to a babysitter, and you would
scream your lungs out for me.*

*It broke my heart to hear you cry like that.
One day, I turned around, scooped you up, and
whispered in your ear. I promised you that I
would be right back as soon as I finished working.*

*I still remember placing my hand over
your little heart while telling you that I'd be "right
in here". Even when you don't see me, I'm right in
there. Don't lose your daddy's medallion, and
don't end up like the two of us. I'ma pray one
more time. Tee, I love you always.*

Mommy

*****

The more tears I wipe away, the more they
run down my face. For the next three or four
hours, I sit on the floor, holding the medallion,
while rocking back and forth. I listen to the sound

of nothingness bouncing off the walls. Eventually, I get up off the floor, but a piece of my soul stays down there. I walk over to the front door, turned around, and take one last look at the apartment that I once called home. I walk out the door, never to return to the eighth floor again.

CHAPTER SEVEN

DEATH IS JUST A PART OF LIFE

TEE

I take the stairs this time. I'm on my way to get Ed's book bag like X had told me to do. Fuck the dog. Fuck everybody. If there is another dog on the staircase, I don't give a fuck.

I reach 4B and knock hard on the door, but it still takes a while for Tuff to open the door.

"What's up, GT?"

"What's up, Tuff?"

Before I even walk into the crib, Des starts with that same old bullshit.

"Look, everybody! It's the garbage room kid. Garbageroomtomb."

As usual, some people laugh, and some don't, but the laughter is short lived because I'm full of pure anger.

"Fuck you, Des, with your bitch ass!"

My words echo throughout the apartment, maybe throughout the whole fourth floor. The look Des has on his face is the same icy look the pit bull had given me on the staircase. I stare right back at his ass for a second or two or until an unknown force pushes his stare through my eyes and out the back of my head. Tuff tosses me Ed's book bag.

"GT, hurry up and take that to X. They looking for ya downstairs."

I catch the book bag and head for the door, but not before a forty ounce bottle of beer flies past my head and explodes on the front door. Beer and glass goes everywhere, especially in my face and on my clothes. I continue out the door and I don't look back to see if Des is following me to finish the job. I hurry home to find X, Ohme, and Ed, sitting at the dining room table playing poker, drinking, and smoking.

Ed put down his cards and stands up from the table.

"What happened to you? We were looking for you, and why you wet? It's raining outside or something?"

He asks me twenty questions before I take two breaths. I fight hard to control my pain and anger, until I finally let it go.

"Nah, it's not raining outside" and, without skipping a beat, I turn to X.

"Is my moms dead?"

A steady stream of tears start rolling down my face again.

"I don't know, Tee. All I know is that she's real sick."

The look on X's face confirms what I already know.

"Shit! I don't believe this shit."

Ohme looks at me for a second. Then, he gets me a towel out of the hallway closet.

"Here. Wipe your face, Tee."

Ohme looks at me real hard for a minute. He looks like he's struggling with what he wants to tell me.

"I know this shit is hard for you right now." He waits for a minute. Then continues, "Let me tell you something about life and death. A caterpillar don't know a damn thing about what it means to be a butterfly. All it knows is that it has to survive in order to weave a cocoon. After that— Boom! — It comes out of the cocoon as a beautiful butterfly. Ain't that some shit? Yesterday, the caterpillar ain't have no wings, but, today, that motherfucker's flying around, seeing life in a totally different way. People don't know shit about what happens after we die. That's the scary part. That's why it hurts like hell when somebody we love has to leave, but death is just a part of life. We just don't know that much about it, but we do know how to survive, and I know ya hurting real bad right now, but you will survive."

With that, Ohme pats me on my shoulder. While Ohme is talking to me, I wipe away the tears and the stink-ass beer. Something Ohme said finally makes sense to me, especially the part about the butterfly, which seems strange because I haven't had a chance to say anything about my pops' medallion. The shit slipped my mind until now.

"I almost forgot. This is what my moms left me."

I pull the medallion out of my pocket and hold it up for them to see.

"It belonged to my pops."

Ed says its dope, but X and Ohme don't say a word. They just look at each other like they just seen a ghost.

"Oh, yeah! Here's your book bag, Ed."

He takes it from me and goes into X's room.

"Why you wet, Tee?"

"That bitch-ass Des threw a forty ounce at me, but I kept my cool, though."

"Yo, Tee. Don't worry about that shit," X reassures me. "I'ma take care of Des. Just go get yourself cleaned up 'cause we ordered pizza."

CHAPTER EIGHT

THE HUSTLE

TEE

The next day and every day after that for about a year, the phone would ring at five A.M. Then, Ed would grab a book bag from under his bed. He would leave the house with it and come back without it. Every day, I would get the book bag from 4B. Sometimes, I would get Ed's book bag twice a day. I knew Ed's ass wasn't going to school. Besides that, we did the book bag thing on Saturdays and Sundays and even on holidays. I didn't mind or ask any questions because X would always say, "Here, Tee. Take your money and go get a book from the library. Don't forget Ed's book bag on your way back."

Every once in a while, Ohme would ask me, "Tee, you read any good books lately?"

Other times, he would hand me a piece of paper with some book title scribbled on it and say,

"I heard it's a good book. You can read it when I'm finished with it."

Sure enough, when Ohme finished reading the damn thing, he would give it to me.

It became safer for me to just read the book because Ohme would ask slick-ass questions or say something that only a person who had read the book would know, and X didn't give me a break either.

"Go get Ed's book bag from upstairs and make sure to ask Des if it's all there. If it's not, you ain't getting your two hundred dollars."

So, I had to learn how to look Des in the face and take care of business. I was no match for Des, but reading all those books must have paid off. I learned how a little manipulation and some mind games helped me deal with Des most of the time anyway, except when he was pissy drunk, real high, or both at the same time. The verbal attacks weren't nothing, but the way he looked at me, sometimes, made the book bag pick up rough.

Everybody else in 4B was cool, though, real cool. It got to the point that, whenever I went to 4B or saw somebody from their crew on the street, they would tell me about who got shot, who got robbed, who was locked up and who was dead. It scared me, sometimes, because some of them would tell me shit that hadn't even happened yet.

One Thursday, I was talking to one dude that I knew was gonna get shot on Saturday.

If person A told me he was going out of town on Monday, person B, his best friend, would tell me he had fucked person A's girlfriend while A was out of town. I never repeated anything I heard. Well, maybe only once.

CHAPTER NINE

UNHAPPY NEW YEAR

TEE

It's New Year's Eve, and it's freezing outside. Me, Ed, Tuff, Shy, and Bam are on the staircase breaking in the New Year. I have a drink or two, so I'm feeling real nice.

"Here, G.T. Roll this up for me."

Tuff pulls a Dutch Master cigar out of his coat pocket and hands it to me.

"I don't know how to roll no spliff," I explain to him as I take the cigar and remove its plastic wrapper.

I've seen people do it all the time, so I figured it can't be that hard. With my thumbnail, I split the cigar down the center, while Tuff breaks up the weed into small crumbs on a twenty dollar bill. Suddenly, the cigar disintegrates in my hand and falls apart on the staircase floor.

"Ah, come on, G.T.! That was the last Dutch," Tuff yells.

"My bad! My bad! I'll go to the store and get another one."

That's the least I could do, seeing how hurt everybody is because the damn Dutch broke. Well, Ed thinks it's funny, but he is not the one going to the store thirty-seven minutes before midnight in the freezing cold.

Damn! How did I fuck that Dutch up? Everybody else makes it look so easy, I wonder as I walk to the store, trying to focus on my steps. I don't want anybody to see how vulnerable I am right now; and all I had was one drink. To make it worse, I'm on edge as the firecrackers and gunshots explode in every direction.

The two holidays that get my blood flowing are the Fourth of July and New Year's Eve. I never know if it's going to be a bottle rocket or a bullet flying pass my head. I make it to the store in one piece. Thank God.

I guess I'm not the only one who had broke a Dutch because the store is packed with people getting cigars, cigarettes, and cheap wine.

As I wait in line, I overhear a couple of dudes talking about Tuff.

"It's about to be 1993, and I'ma start robbing these motherfuckers up the block," says one of the dudes as he places a cheap bottle of wine on the counter.

"Yeah, I be seeing them with their jewels, pulling out money like shit is sweet," the other one says.

I think the last one says, "Let's get Tuff."

I'm not sure, but I hear something close to that. My first thought is *They got to be joking.* My second thought is *They have to know about me, Tuff, and the 3B crew. If I act like I'm scared, they gonna rob me, and, if I stay here any longer, I'm gonna faint.* I try to stay calm, but I can't. I walk out the store with my head down. Then, I run as fast as I can up the block. When I get back to the building, I run into the house and tell the first person I see.

Ohme is on the couch waiting for the New Year's ball to drop.

"Ohme, there's some dudes at the store, talking about robbing Tuff, and I think they was gonna rob me, too."

"8...7...6...5...4...3...2...1! Happy New Year!" rings out from the TV screen.

He stands up and tells me to come with him.

"Hold up. Where's X?"

I had seen the characters we were up against and know we need all the help we can get.

"X is in the room, knocked out," Ohme answers.

I walk my ass towards X's room, but Ohme tells me to "let X sleep and come on".

In the hallway, I try again.

"You want me to go get Ed, Tuff, and them? I know where they at."

"Hell no!"

Ohme makes it seem like a bad idea. We make our way downstairs to Ohme's car. I'm shook, and all I can think about is all the things that can go wrong. Ohme, on the other hand, isn't Ohme no more. His face is different. His eyes are now a deep black abyss. We drive up the block and pass the store, but I don't see the guys that had tried to get me. Ohme circles the block and parks the car. We sit there, watching every face that comes from every direction. I finally spot two of the three dudes walking back to the store.

"There goes two of them right there," I reluctantly tell Ohme.

I slouch down in my seat, just a little, as Ohme takes a quick glance. After that, we drive back to our building.

"Alright, Tee. Don't worry about that shit. I know them cats. I'll be back soon. Go 'head. Go upstairs."

Before I get to the building entrance, he calls me.

"Yo, Tee!"

I turn around.

"Happy New Year!"

Then, he drives away.

I run upstairs to see if X is awake or if Ed has come home yet. Both are a negative, so I go back to the staircase where the crew is at. Shy and Bam are gone, but Ed and Tuff are still hanging out.

"Damn, Tee! What took you so long?" Ed asks.

Tuff extends his hand with the twenty dollar bill still containing the weed.

"Roll up."

"Some dudes just tried to rob me, and they was talking about robbing you, too."

"Well, they better hurry up 'cause I'm 'bout to spend my money on a new car. That's my New Year's resolution," Tuff jokes, or maybe he's serious. You never know with Tuff.

"I told Ohme, and he went out there after them by himself."

"Shit" is all Tuff says as he gets up and staggers down the stairs.

I watch him disappear behind the banister of the stairwell, and I can hear his footsteps as he jumps down the steps. Finally, I hear the echo of the door slam from the lower level of the staircase.

"Yo, Ed! We gotta do something. Ohme's out there for self."

Ed sits there, drunk as fuck, mumbling, "Ohme don't need no help, Ohme don't need nobody. You need to be worried about Tuff's drunk ass. That motherfucker's stupid."

I can't sit here not knowing what is going on in the streets.

"I'm going back to the crib, you coming?" I ask.

"Nah, I'ma chill here for a while and drink the rest of this liquor."

I go into the house and try to watch some TV. I think about waking X, but now feel like a real punk. Am I the only one who gives a shit?

Later, in the night, Ohme wakes me up and tells me to get out his spot and to go to bed.

"Yo! What happened? You alright?"

"Yeah. I'm alright. I told you not to worry about it."

I drag my ass to bed, not giving the situation another thought. That is until I go to the library a couple of days later. I pass by the corner store only to see broken yellow tape dangling in the wind. As I got closer to the carnage, I see dried blood stains on the sidewalk. I don't know what had happened, and I don't want to know. From now on, I think it's better if I keep my mouth shut.

CHAPTER TEN

BRAIN FOOD

TEE

The librarians are used to seeing me now and they know why I'm here, unlike most of the kids that come to the library to get out of the cold or the heat. They can goof off and get thrown out on their asses but me personally; I enjoy leaving this world every time I open a book.

"Give me all your money."

I jump and turn around to see Tuff standing in line behind me with a book in his hand.

"Yo! Stop playing! What happened to you the other night?"

I knew damn well that, whatever had happened, Tuff wasn't about to tell me.

"Did you see the blood in front of the store?"

"Yeah. That was crazy," Tuff answers in that casual way of his.

I want to know what happened, but I think, *I already know*. Besides, my conscious can't hold any more secrets. I leave it alone and change the subject.

"Yo, Tuff! Why, every time I see you, it looks like you going to a club?"

"'Cause every day I'm living is a cause for celebration. Plus, if I die, I want to look good doing it."

"That's stupid 'cause, if you dead, why do you care what people think?"

"That's just it. I don't care what they think; I just feel better knowing that I'll look fly when I die. I can't beat death, but I can beat looking like shit when it gets me."

We both bust out laughing.

"You a funny dude, Tuff. What you doing in the library?"

"Brain food, baby. The mind, body, and soul gotta eat."

That's what I like about this dude. He doesn't try to be hard or cool. He just is and somehow he still finds a way to enjoy life at the same damn time.

"Hey, Tuff. You going back to the building?"

"Yeah. I'm heading back that way."

"Alright. I'ma wait for you. I gotta get Ed's book bag anyway."

We walk the few, long blocks back to our block. It takes even longer than usual because every couple of steps, I stop to laugh at something Tuff has said.

"G.T., can I ask you something without you getting mad?"

"You can ask me anything you want as long as you stop calling me that name. I hate that. My name is Tee."

"Oh, my bad, Tee! I know you fought that dog, but was he really trying to kill you? I mean, I know he attacked you, but was it really as bad as they say it was?"

Before I answer Tuff's questions, I think hard about the details of that day. I had buried most of my pain in my subconscious a long time ago.

"You motherfuckin' right that bitch tried to kill me!"

I stopped walking and look at him in disbelief.

"Did they tell you it killed a little kid that day?"

The memory of the whole ugly mess comes back to me and, for a second, I hate Tuff for bringing it up.

"Why you bringing that dumb shit up for?"

Tuff opens his mouth to speak, but, before he can, we hear somebody calling us.

From across the street, Ed is coming out the corner store, hollering at us.

"Yo, G.T.! Tuffy! Yo, Tuff!"

He runs over to catch up with us.

"Son, I don't got no blood on my sneakers, do I?"

He lifts up his feet, one at a time, to show us the bottom of his shoes.

"Nah, I don't see nothing," Tuff said as I shake my head.

"Did y'all see?"

"Yeah, we saw," Tuff answers as I nod my head. We laugh as we all walk back to our building.

With all the money I have coming in now, I ask Tuff to take me to the same store that he gets his clothes from. And it was really on when Tuff takes me to a guy he knows that works in a jewelry store. I buy a chain for my butterfly medallion and I got the missing cubic zirconium put back in. From this day on, I'm going to walk around looking like my pops and shit.

CHAPTER ELEVEN

HAPPY BIRTHDAY, TEE!

ED

It's G.T.'s sixteenth birthday, and the plan is to drop off the book bag, get dressed in our flyest shit, and then go catch an early matinee at the movies. If we have enough time, we can go shopping, but we definitely have to make time for some curry chicken at my favorite Jamaican restaurant.

Tuff is supposed to come with us, but he hasn't shown up yet. I guess that he has other plans.

I don't really give a fuck if he shows or not, it's Tee's stupid ass that's disappointed, but not for long. No, buddy.

When I saw the sixteen hundred dollars X and Ohme gave G.T. for a birthday present, it wasn't hard to convince me to be a chaperone, even though I'm only a year older. If we do it right, we can go have a good time and still make it back in time for G.T.'s book bag pick up. Everything is going according to plan until we get to the lobby of the building. At the front door to the lobby, we see two detectives and two uniformed cops banging on the lobby door. One of the cops has the nerve to point at me and then at the door. Now, if I want to be on some gangsta shit, I can insult their asses through the door, run back upstairs or to another exit before they get in the lobby, but I decide to keep my cool and open the door. I even hold the shit open for them. Instead of a thank you, I get a bunch of fucking questions.

"Hey! Where y'all coming from? You live here? What floor you live on?"

They asked twenty-one questions without stopping to take a single breath. I respond with a quick but smart answer, if I must say so myself.

"I'm not suppose to talk to strangers, and you're welcome for me opening the door for you."

The DT grabs me by the shirt and slams me against the wall.

"You want to fucking go to jail?"

The other cops walk off like they didn't just see that shit.

I came back with another smart-ass answer.

"If it means I get to eat tonight, then, yeah, I'll go."

He looks at me like he wants to slap the shit out of me and I look at him like I want to be slapped.

Maybe it's G.T.'s pitiful-looking ass in the corner he's feeling sorry for, or he might be telling himself, *What a fucked up country we live in, when a kid would go to jail just to get a free meal.* Then again, that would require deep thought, and this one is not a deep thinker.

"Hey, Joe! Let's go," the other DT calls to his partner.

"Both of you, get the fuck out of here before you end up eating free meals and getting raped for the next six months in juvie, you little bastards."

He lets go of my shirt and looks me up and down.

"Have a nice day," he says and walks off to catch up with his boy.

"G.T.! G.T.! Let's go!"

I hurry G.T. out of the building, so we can enjoy ourselves like we planned.

I think G.T. had a good time, except for the beef we got into. Some kids were scheming on G.T.'s chain. Luckily, I was there. All G.T. did was give them a cold Des look. I, on the other hand, lifted up my shirt and showed off my baby nine. Damn right, I had it all the time that dumb fuck was harassing me back at the building.

Anyway, there were seven or eight dudes plotting on snatching G.T.'s chain. Even after I flashed my piece, some of them still wanted to go for it. The butterfly medallion looks that damn tempting. I wasn't going to make it easy for them without a mess. A big mess, looking back on it. We kept it moving while watching everything and everybody around us.

When we return to the building, we go up to 4B to pick up the book bag.

It takes them a while to open the door, but finally they let us in.

"What's up? What's up?"

Me and G.T. greet out as we walk in with our shopping bags.

Everybody seems to be in their own little world. Des is the first one to speak from his seat on the raggedy-ass couch.

"Y'all know your boy is dead, right?"

"Who? Who?" G.T. asks it a little faster than me, but we answered almost at the same time.

"Tuff is dead, yo." Only a cold-blooded motherfucker like Des could say it like that.

I watch G.T.'s eyes water up, so my eyes water up, too.

"What happened?" I ask, but nobody is sure.

All I can piece together from the 4B crew is that somebody killed him and his dog. Then, they tossed their bodies into the ninth floor garbage room. Who could do that to my boy? Tuff was the coolest dude I knew. It probably was some dudes up the block or maybe he had fucked somebody's girl. Who knows? A knock on the door makes everyone freeze and stop talking.

We look at each other to see which one of us will answer the door. Soon, the knock on the door is replaced with a sharp bang on the door. The 4B crew are on edge, and I don't understand why. I mean, Tuff was my man, but people die every day.

"G.T., get the door!" Des yells, giving the order like we still live up in this bitch or something.

G.T. looks through the peep hole and opens the door quickly. It's X and Ohme. I'm not scared of nobody, but the look in Ohme's eyes aint a good one. He walks in and called everyone into the living room. X walks in after him and takes a seat on the couch next to Des. X doesn't say a word.

"Is this it? Everybody here?" Ohme asks.

Before I can blink, he pulls out his gun and points it at our heads one by one.

That's fucked up, if you ask me. *Why he ain't pointing that shit at X and G.T.? And why he got to point it at me, though?* No one moves, and no one says a word. He rotates his arm around the room like the hands on a clock. Somebody needs to do something before he kills somebody up in here. This fool done went crazy.

I have to say something 'cause nobody else is saying nothing. I mean, I don't care if he shoots Des's ass, but I don't want to see him kill nobody else, especially me.

"Chill, Ohme. It was probably them dudes up the block that killed Tuff."

Ohme continues to point his gun at us, "That was my man right there. That was like my little brother."

Ohme's full attention finally goes to Des. He licks his lips while taking aim. X slowly stands up and steps in front of the weapon. Ohme's gun, X's stomach, and Des's head are now in perfect alignment. I hold my breath, and everything stops, like someone has pushed the pause button on the VCR.

CHAPTER TWELVE

WE OUT

TEE

"I got ten Gs," X announces. "Ten grand for whoever finds out who killed Tuff."

Des peeks out from around X's body and says, "And the dog. I want to know who killed the dog, too."

I say to myself, *Tee, something ain't right*. I search the eyes of everyone in the room because it was no coincidence that Tuff and the dog had gotten killed in the garbage room. I feel like someone is sending me a message. Suddenly, I look at Des. He looks back at me, and I swear I see a small grin on his face. It causes me to look away quickly.

Right in the nick of time, X starts to speak again.

"This building is hot, so the third floor crew is going on vacation. I suggest you all do the same. If not, handle your business, but, if you get locked up, you don't fucking know me."

I notice the mood change in the room. While I can picture Tuff, lying dead on top of a fucking dog in the garbage room, other people are whispering about the ten Gs, and how they can't possibly survive without X and Ohme's unbeatable drug prices.

When we get back down to 3B, I can't bite my tongue any longer.

"Yo, Ohme! I think Des did that shit to Tuff."

Ohme never responds. He just goes into X's room and slams the door.

"Anything's possible," X says, "but I don't think he did it. When me and Des were kids, nobody could stand his ass, not even me. The other kids were putting the beats on him. He was getting teased and robbed every day."

"What? Des used to get beat up and robbed?"

I'm shocked. I put on the same grin Des had given me upstairs.

"Don't laugh," X says. "That just made him meaner, tougher, and crazier. One day, I was coming back from the store, when this crazy looking pit bull started to follow me home."

The smile on my face disappears.

"Was you scared?"

I hate the thought of being the only one in the world who is scared of dogs.

"I was scared as hell," X answered. "I mean this pit was the toughest looking motherfucker I had ever seen. He was all black and had about a hundred scars on his face. You would have thought he had been in a war or something, so I stood real still as I tried to decide whether I was going to run for it or fight for my life."

"That shit bit the shit out of you, didn't it?" Ed asked while he tried to hold back a smirk.

"Nah, he didn't bite me; he licked my hand. I looked down at this punk-ass dog, and he looked back at me like a baby, looking for a bottle. I bullshit you not. I fell in love with that dog. I decided to call him Blackbaby. When I got back to the block, everybody was laughing at me because I had this mangy pit with me. Everybody but Des, that is. He was all over Blackbaby, fleas and everything. Before the day was over, he was in love with Blackbaby, too."

"Wait! Wait! Wait! Des loved something? I can't believe Des is capable of loving anything or anybody."

"Yo! I'm telling you. Des loved that dog to death. We kept the dog in the backyard behind the building until one of us could bring him home. That was the plan anyway, but, when I asked my pops, he just looked at me, so I knew what that meant— HELL NO! Des took Blackbaby home and hid him in the closet. His mother found Blackbaby and brought him to my house. She tried to sell my dog to my father for some coke. I saw my pops give her the same look he gave me."

Ohme comes back out of X's room and sits down on the couch, while X continues the story.

"Des and I ran away that day. We hit the streets hard. We begged and stole just to eat and feed Blackbaby. The shit seems funny now, but I swear to God, we would have starved as long as Blackie ate. Every day or two, I would go home, clean myself up, and steal some food out the refrigerator. My pops would smile at me, like I had told him a joke or something. The crazy thing about it is Des never went home. He stayed on the streets, dirty, hungry, and desperate. That's when I realized we had no choice but to hustle. We had to do something fast because winter was coming, and it gets cold out there, cold enough to kill you."

"Is that how Blackbaby died? He froze to death," Ed asks.

"Nah, before you knew it, Blackbaby was eating better than some people I knew. We even had enough money to get our own place. Everybody on this planet has a weakness for something, so, once we found out what the landlord had a taste for, we worked something out and got the apartment. All the kids on the block wanted to hang out in our crib. That's where I met my man Ohme, right there."

"So, what happened to Blackbaby?" Ed interrupts again.

"Some dudes must have got jealous of us because someone started shooting at Des one night when he was walking Blackbaby. Des ain't get hit, but Blackbaby caught it. He died right in Des's arms."

X takes a deep breath and stares off into another world.

"Nah, I don't think Des did it. I even tried to give him a baby pit bull to replace Blackbaby, but he took it straight upstairs and gave him to Tuff's uncle."

X drifted off to that other world again, but just for a second.

"Enough about that. We leaving tomorrow. Bring your money and pack some summer shit. We out!"

I wake up early the next morning, but apparently not early enough.

"Hurry up, Tee. We ready to go. Why you so damn slow?"

Ohme has never yelled at me before. I want to remind him that I, of all people, knew how he was feeling right now. It wasn't that long ago that I had lost Moms, and it was Ohme who had known just what to say. I started to say something to him, but, when he looked at the butterfly medallion hanging from my neck, he seemed to calm down.

I got a little attitude as I struggle with my two bags and a sneaker box. Everybody is gone except for X, who standing at the front door waiting for me. Ed is already standing at the elevator with his bags, while Ohme is beside him with a big suitcase similar to X's.

The whole time in the elevator, the whole time in the lobby, as well as the whole time on the street, X and Ohme argue about whose car we should use.

Finally, Ohme tells X, "If we take your car, then you driving."

X and Ohme take turns driving X's car. It's the longest trip I have ever taken in my life. Hell! I've never been two miles out of the neighborhood.

During the ride, Ed spends most of the time talking in his sleep. I move closer to him to try and figure out what he is saying but give up when I notice he's drooling on his shirt. I spend the rest of the time looking out the car window, enjoying the sights.

I have never seen so many trees, and the clouds looked like somebody had spray painted them in the sky. As we pass through different cities and different towns, I try to imagine what other people were doing. I can't help but wonder if there are other kids with the same problems as me. Have they been forgotten and thrown away like me? Are they hurting like me? Have they written their wills before the age of sixteen like me?

It seems like the scenery stays the same most of the time.

Ed wakes up, and I doze off. Ed dozes off, and I wake up. X drives; then Ohme drives. After each snooze, I jump up like a paranoid drug addict and try to see if there is anything new to look at.

All of a sudden, I sit up straight and blink my eyes to make sure I'm not dreaming. Sure enough, nothing but palm trees, one after another, after another. Off in the distance, I can see waves of water rolling up to the sand. This is the kind of stuff I had only seen on TV or read about in books. They say "seeing is believing", and now I'm sure this vacation is going to be off the chain.

Finally, we pull up to a gate. It looks like housing projects for rich people. The houses are connected to each other, and they keep on going for as far as the eyes can see. Beyond that, I can see the beach and the endless ocean water. In the distance, I can almost see the image of an amusement park, roller coaster, and all of that.

At the gate, Ohme whips out some official looking papers and hands them to the guard. The security guard at the gate has that "there goes the neighborhood" look on his face. He seems to read the paper work four or five times, but, after a few minutes more of the bullshit, he hands Ohme a parking sticker and opens the gate.

The villa suite is cool, but, in my opinion, 3B is better. The first floor of the villa is bigger than the entire third floor apartment. The suite has an upstairs level with three bedrooms. Each bedroom has a big bed and a big TV. The bathrooms are equipped with walk in showers and marble floors.

I play around with the water jets on the wall until X walks in and jokingly says, "Either get the fuck in or turn the shower off. We gotta pay for water here."

I quickly turn the water off and unpack my bags. When I return downstairs, I go out the back door and find myself staring at the flyest backyard I have ever seen. There's patio furniture and a golf cart parked on the side of the house.

"Oh, shit! Everybody got a golf cart in their backyard," Ed says so loud that he probably scares the old folks next door.

Back in the house, I notice that the kitchen and living room are divided by a huge curved counter with barstools on the living room side of the room.

"Our shit back home is better," I say out loud this time, but, surprisingly enough, no one agrees with me.

Ohme sits down on the huge sofa sectional and watches TV like always. I know where he's sleeping tonight.

"Ed! Tee! Come here!"

X calls us and opens up a small black book.

"Both of you made a lot of money, so you should be straight with money."

X, then, turns to an empty page in the book and writes down the address to the suite, plus a four digit password.

"This password will let you get into any gate around this complex."

X rips the paper out the book and hands it to me.

"If you lose this paper, you assed out. Punch in the four digit code and the pound key to get in and out the gates."

"Where the gates at?" I ask because I'm worried about getting lost in this big-ass place.

"They got gates all over the place," X says. "They got a beach across the street and an amusement park."

I smile when I hear about the amusement park, but X doesn't stop there.

"There's also a mall and a museum. Man, when I came out here last time, they had a zoo up the block with lions and tigers and bears and shit."

"You been out here before?" Ed asks.

"Yeah. A long time ago. Hey, look! If y'all get hungry, they got restaurants everywhere around here."

As usual, Ohme says some off the wall shit, too.

"Be careful out here 'cause it ain't where you from, it's where you at. The whole world is a ghetto, and it be like that."

Ohme is on a roll now, kicking a freestyle from off the top of his head.

"They got rich people, poor people, living in hell. You better watch all people, so you come home well."

Ohme starts to loosen up a bit, but I can tell Tuff's murder is still eating him up alive. Street life makes you angry and ready for war, twenty-four hours a day, seven days a week, three hundred and sixty-five days a year. Hopefully, you catch a breather. Hopefully, you get a good night's sleep. Hopefully, you get to live, but not too much. According to Ohme, the caterpillar can't fully live until it gets its wings. The butterfly has to be full of hope when it closes its eyes as a caterpillar.

Ohme throws the keys to the suite to Ed as he and X walk out, jump in the car, and haul ass.

I look at Ed and ask, "Where the fuck they going?"

Ed stands there for a minute with his mouth open. Then, he says, "Man, fuck them. I got twenty, maybe twenty-two thousand dollars, in my bag."

"That's cool Ed, I got about forty four thousand upstairs."

Ed looks real confused now. He's been hustling longer than me, so how the hell do I got so much more than him? He should've listened to me when I told him to stop spending all his money on weed and liquor. I had been listening to Ohme, even though, sometimes, he talks that crazy shit. In reality, I have almost a hundred thousand dollars total. Ohme is holding the rest of my money for safe keeping. I don't tell Ed this, though. Ohme would also say, "Don't never let nobody know what you holding, kid." X and Ohme know what I'm holding because it's their business to know. At two hundred dollars a day, fourteen hundred dollars a week, fifty-six hundred dollars a month, sixty-seven thousand dollars a year for two years, minus expenses and dumb shit I feel I had to have, I'm not doing bad at all.

Ed and I have two choices. We can put our money in a book bag and take it with us, or we can hide it. We decide to hide it because had left his heater at home.

"Ed. I got just the spot."

I take Ed upstairs to my bathroom and take the top off the toilet bowl tank. Inside the tank, I had a huge Ziploc bag with my money in it. I put it in there when I unpacked my bags. I take three thousand dollars out of my stash, and Ed does the same. We count his money before mixing his with mine. After hiding our money, we decide to go out. When we get to the front door, Ed remembers the golf cart, so we go out the back door instead.

He locks the door, turns to me, and asks, "So, what you want to do first?"

"The amusement park. We gotta do the amusement park."

My mind was set on the amusement park from when we first pulled up to the villa

Without saying another word, we jump into the golf cart and drive it to the far end of the complex. It makes our walk to the amusement park a short one.

The roller coaster ride went left to right. It twisted. It took us high, then low. It took us fast, then slow. It was a perfect reflection of my ghetto life.

Me and Ed spent the whole day and night on the rides. We walked up and down the boardwalk, eating, laughing, and talking about the simplest little things we observed going on around us.

"Yo, G.T.! Look at that lady," He shows no shame as he points out a lady with an orange hat and red bathing suit on.

"Ed, look!"

I pull on his shirt and point at a seagull as it snatches a hot dog right out of some kid's hand. At two A.M., the park begins to shut down for the night.

"This shit was fun. I'm coming back tomorrow," I tell him.

He agrees to come back the next day, too, because we didn't even get to go on all the rides. On the long walk back to the gate where we had parked the golf cart, we talk about the good time we'd had.

Suddenly, I turn to Ed, "You know you're my best friend, right?"

Without breaking stride, Ed responds, "Shit! You my only friend, G.T," and we both bust out laughing just like we'd been doing all day.

For the first two days, we spent all of our time at the amusement park, sometimes going on the same ride two or three times, and playing games to win prizes. Ed won thirteen stuffed animals, and I won ten. It even took me two hours and one hundred and thirty-six dollars to win a boom box that I had to have. The funny thing is, we didn't even want the stuffed animals, and, after a while, we ended up giving them away to some little kids and a couple of old people we met along the way.

Every day, we found something new to do or somewhere new to go. We barely spent time at the suite, and we barely saw X and Ohme. Some days, we would go to the zoo and try to imagine what the animals were thinking about. How did they feel about their lives? Did they believe in God? Crazy shit like that, knowing we would never know the answer. On another day, we went to the mall and shopped for clothes and I ended up having the zirconium in my medallion replaced with real diamonds.

One day, at the museum, I was giving Ed a history lesson about the ancient Sumerians.

"Ed, this ain't nothing. I read a book one time about the first known civilization. These people invented the wheel and came up with mathematics and all kinds of other stuff."

He's not impressed until I explain: "If you read some of the books I've read, you would be amazed. Before Noah and the flood, angels were having sex with human women, and their children came out like giants and God-like monsters."

Now, I got his attention. He's not looking at the statues and paintings on the wall no more.

"This is where the shit gets crazy, Ed. God was pissed, so He flooded the whole world. Then, after that, God cleaned house in heaven. He kicked out some of his angels, some of His children. It didn't matter who you was. The moral of the story is 'no matter how great you think you are, there can be only one big baller, one shot caller,' and that's a fact."

Ed is skeptical about my story, so he asks, "You think that shit really happened?"

I laugh and respond, "I asked Ohme the same thing, and he said, 'I don't know, but, according to every religion and every civilization in the world, something happened.'"

We laugh and continue looking at some of the meaningless but priceless items in the museum.

On the last day of vacation, Ed finally talks me into going to the beach. We sit on the hot sand and stare into the clear blue water. Ed pours crystal sand into his hand and lets it slip between his fingers. Meanwhile, I bury my feet and scarred ankles in the sand. My arms and ankles have permanent reminders of the pit bull attack.

"One day, Tee, I'm coming back here."

"I wish I could come back here, too, Ed, but it probably costs mad dough to live out here."

I'm not trying to bust his bubble, but this is not the place for two young hustlers. Honestly speaking, most people work their whole lives just for a one week vacation in a place like this.

"We need big money like X to live in a place like this. No offense, but we book bag runners,"

I tell him.

"Yo! Let me tell you something, Tee. You think Ohme ain't chip in for this shit?"

Ed's dream slips away like the sand in his hand.

"Tee, I'm telling you. If we team up, we can take over the whole block when we get back."

"Ed, I don't know nothing about hustling. I don't even want to hustle. I like picking up book bags and staying out of real danger, to tell you the truth. Do you know how many friends I've lost in 4B?"

"What the fuck you think we've been picking up and dropping off? You think its books in them book bags?"

I can sense Ed's anger. His dream goes from slipping out of his hand to slipping into the deep, vast sea.

"You think we a fucking library on wheels or something?"

"Hold up, Ed. You act like I'm stupid or something. I know what's up with the book bags.

I'm just saying, we make good money. Ain't no need to get greedy."

As Ed calms down, he is able to take heed of my calm, cool reasoning.

"Besides, I know you don't want to get robbed, locked up, or killed by some psychopath motherfucker like Des."

Ed jumps up from the sand and looks at me. His eyes turn red with anger, blood red.

"Yo! Fuck Des!"

Ed is now madder than before.

"I'm gonna run that block one day. You gonna see. Watch! I'm coming back here to live lovely. Watch! Just watch me!"

The crazy look in his eyes beat out Des's look, surpassed even the look the pit bull had given me in the staircase. This boy had done lost his mind. I want to laugh but decide against it.

That night, we start our long ride back home. Back home to where the hustling is. Back home to Des and his bullshit. Back home to a whole lot of shit brewing and then some. Little did we know that the hell we were going back to was even hotter than it was when we had left it.

CHAPTER THIRTEEN

HOTTER THAN WE LEFT IT

X

Me and Ohme take turns driving my car back home. It's a long sixteen hour ride. When we finally arrive back at the apartment, I'm dead tired but recharged at the same time.

Ohme walks up to the door, takes out his key, and puts it into the lock. He turns the knob and opens the door. Ohme pulls out his heat and steps inside. I look at him like he's crazy until I replay his every step in my mind. It then, dawns on me, he never turned the key. The door was unlocked. I was thrown off-guard but come to my senses quickly. I immediately pull my heat out like a washed up gunslinger. I tell Tee and Ed to "shhh" as I follow Ohme into the apartment. The first thing I notice is my back— nobody has it. Ed and Tee are standing still at the front door, as I go right and Ohme goes left into the apartment.

A strong, cool breeze from a broken window in the living room hits my body. The black curtains no longer hang from the window; now, they cover the floor. I see that the entertainment center has dust sitting where the big TV used to be. My couch and loveseat are cut up and torn apart. My two lion statues are now in a thousand pieces on the floor. The huge stereo speakers must have been a figment of my imagination because they damn sure aren't there now. I made my way to the kitchen where our food has been tossed all over the floor. My refrigerator is also lying on its side. Both bedrooms have been ransacked, and our mattresses are flipped and sliced into.

After we creep through the rest of the crib and make sure that everything is okay, I tell Tee and Ed to come in.

All the closets are empty and everything in them is either missing or on the floor. Last but not least, everything in the bathroom is on the floor. Even the top to the toilet bowl tank has been smashed to pieces.

Somebody had used the fire escape to break into our crib. It didn't take a genius to figure that out. I can't put my feelings into words, but what Ohme says next says it all, "Damn! I left a slice of pizza in the fridge, too. I was thinking about that pizza the whole time we was driving back."

"It would have been nice if it had still been here, but it's not, so fuck it." Ohme was not ready to understand how anyone but him would want that slice of pizza, but he had to just accept it.

"Yo, Ohme! You know what I want to know?"

"What?"

"How the hell they get them speakers out of here? Remember how hard it was to get them shits in here?"

Ohme points at me and says, "You're right. You're absolutely right."

Ed and Tee's reactions are different from ours. Well, let's just say I see disgust, anger, and weakness. Oh, yeah. I see something else, too. Fear is written all over their faces.

"Tee, you alright?"

"Nah, the smell of the rotten food is putting me in a bad place."

Ed is busy kicking shit that has already been kicked over and breaking shit that's already been broken. He curses and yells all the way to his bedroom.

"What the fuck? This is some bullshit! Hold up! Hold the fuck up! Y'all motherfuckers is talking about pizza and how they got the speakers out of here. These motherfuckers done took my heat, my weed. They even got...my...Hold up! Hell fucking no!"

Ed flips his dresser back to its upright position and rummages through all his belongings on the floor. He looks like a homeless man digging for cans in the trash.

"What's wrong? Yo! What happened?" I ask.

Me and Tee didn't know what to think. I figure they had got him for his money or something.

Tee ask him, "They got your jewelry or something?"

Ed stands straight up, "My journal's gone."

He bends back down. His body language says he's full of disappointment and defeat. He doesn't want to believe it's gone. He needs to believe it's the stress and excitement of the situation that is blurring his vision, so he starts searching again.

Tee tells a joke, similar to the joke me and Ohme had made about the pizza and the speakers.

"Journal? I didn't even know you could write, you big dummy!"

Ed stands up one more time and charges over the tossed mattresses and empty bedrail. He grabs Tee by the throat with both hands. Ed's momentum pushes both of them into the open closet and onto the empty closet floor.

I walk fast, but I don't run to break it up I give both players a chance to score a shot. I can't tell you who won right now, but let's just say, just because you won, don't mean you won.

By the time Ohme gets to the room, he can tell by the look on my face that he had missed a good one, the same way I can tell by the expression on his face that he had wanted to see it. Ohme takes the grown up approach by making them squash the beef. He takes it a step further and said, "Since you'll got so much energy, you'll can clean all this shit up."

After the fight, we never talked about it again. Well, me and Ohme do. I tell Ohme, later that night, I think the fight made them respect each other more. His response is sad but true. "Man deserves no peace. It aint over."

*****

The next day, I called the super and tell him that the window needs to be fixed. Once the window is fixed, we can put in a window gate. Surprisingly, the super comes up and fixes the broken window on the same day I call. Shit! He better had, because his punk ass was probably the one who robbed the crib in the first place.

Tee asks me, "Who do you think did this?"

"To tell you the truth shorty, it could have been friends, could have been enemies, or it could have been strangers. As far as I'm concerned, everybody and anybody did it." This wasn't the first time this had happened to me, but I was going to fucking make sure it was the last time. I had said that the last time it happened too, so I don't know what I'm lying for.

We clean up the apartment and pick up the pieces. Ed is still heated, while Tee is concerned about the book bag pickups. Once you started hustling, it's hard to stop. The hustlers are just as addicted as the addicts. I finally get Tee to shut up when I announce we would be going to visit Biggs in jail.

"I don't do jail visits," Ed announces.

I can't blame him because I really don't want to go either. I had gone to see my pops in jail one time before, and I said I would never go back. I had shed a tear the last time I'd seen him too. No, never again. I refuse to cry up in that motherfucker, but, when we arrived at the prison and when I see his face, the tears drop.

First, they are tears of joy because I haven't seen him in a long-ass time. They, then, become tears of sadness, and those motherfuckers are the worst 'cause they hurt. It's hard to look at this great, powerful man who has been reduced down to a mere human being, just like the rest of us. Time and age has snuck up on him. I'm sad for us both because, if this man can't escape mortality, then I know I'm doomed. He still has that same confident walk, and everyone else seems to disappear when he enters the room. He takes a seat and smiles at me.

"What's up, Pops?" I asked. "How you doing?"

"I'm surviving. I'm living. Sometimes, I'm even happy."

He allows a little laugh to surface. He leans forward in the chair and stroked his salt and pepper beard. Then, he speaks again.

"Listen. Why you waited so long before you came to see me? No. Don't even answer that. I know you don't like coming up here, and I really don't like you seeing me in this place anyway."

"Look, Pops. I'ma keep it real with you. I don't like coming up here 'cause I think they gonna keep me for some shit I did, and, to tell you the truth, it breaks my fucking heart seeing you like this."

"Okay. So, why don't you get on the phone when I'm talking to Ohme? What's the problem?"

"I do be talking to you sometimes. Other times, I really don't got a lot to say. I be telling myself, 'As soon as I do something to make him proud of me, I'll talk to him.'"

"X, cut the shit. I was proud of you before you could walk and before your ass could talk. I don't even have to see you or hear you, and I'm still proud of you."

I go blank. For the first time in my life, I feel weak. I feel like I'm not hard. I feel like I just got a hundred on my test, nothing wrong.

"I'm proud of you, too, Pops. I always have been. I know you got a couple of more years, but I want you to come check out my new restaurant when you get out."

"Restaurant, huh? I'm digging that," Biggs nods approvingly.

"Well, will you do that? Will you come check me?"

"Definitely. I'ma definitely come check you."

My pops looks at Ohme. Then, he looks at Tee and asks, "Who's that little gangsta you got with you?"

"Oh, that's the future right there. Tee, meet my pops. Pops, this is Tee from the eighth floor of our building."

"What's up, little gangster? You live in my building, huh?"

"Yes, sir, Mr. Biggs. Born and raised. My mother's name was Mona, and my dad's name was Carl. They dead now, though."

My pops told Tee to come closer to him. "Look me in my eyes, Tee. Which one of these two do you like more— X or Ohme?"

Tee jumps back in surprise, cracks a smile, and says, "I don't know. I guess I like them the same."

My pops motions for Tee to come closer to him again. Then, he said, "People come and go. You love, and you lose, but, if you had to lose one, which one would you let go?"

Tee sits there, stuck in the chair, the same way I would be stuck when he used to ask me questions like that.

"Both of them! Mr. Biggs, I would rather let both of them go at the same time," Tee responds.

My pops smiles, and said, "That's right, Tee. Me and you are a lot alike. See, you're smarter than both of them because neither one of them understood that one. Now, I got some business to take care of with Ohme here, but it was nice meeting you, Tee. You can come back and see me anytime."

"Yes, sir, Mr. Biggs. I'll try."

"And, X, you need to come back and see me, too. Can you make sure I get my own table when you open your restaurant?"

"I got you, Pops. I got you."

Me and Tee walk out of the visitors' room, leaving my pops and Ohme behind, so they could discuss some business. I didn't know if it was wishful thinking, and I decided I would ask Ohme as soon as I saw him, but I thought I had heard my pops say he loved me. I thought that was what he had said.

He had finally played his part.

CHAPTER FOURTEEN

YOUR KID COULD WIND UP IN THE GARBAGE

OHME

"Now that they're gone, I really need to talk to you."

"Yo, Biggs! You took me under your wing and treated me like a son, man. I took a little dude under my wing and treated him like a son, and they killed him. I feel like that shit was my fault. You told me to keep my cool. You warned me shit could go bad. Well, shit's gone bad, and I ain't cool with it. I'm going crazy."

Biggs was never the type to get emotional, so I'm not expecting him to feel where I'm coming from. I don't think nobody feels what I feel. If I didn't know any better, I would think that God took the time out to personally slap me in my face by killing Tuff.

Biggs scratches his head and says, "You think you got it bad?"

I don't answer. I can't. He doesn't give me time to.

"I never told you this before, Ohme, but I watched as my father was killed. They hung him from a tree, and, when he was dead, they cut him down and burned him. I was seven years old. What could I do? I was in hell. That's why, when you see heaven in your face, you grab it. Ohme. I want you to take the money you holding for me and put it towards the restaurant."

"Nah, Biggs. We got everything under control. All your money is sitting, waiting for you when you get out of here."

"No!" Biggs answers defiantly. "There's something strange going on in our lives I want you to take my money and open a chain of restaurants. You know what to do, but you can't tell X about our business arrangement."

Once again, he got me. When I was younger, while everybody else was nickel and diming it, I was responsible for supplying the drugs and being a guardian angel over his kid. Now, I was going to be responsible for my restaurant and, knowing Biggs, probably twenty restaurants across the city.

"I know how you feel," he tells me. "You think I'm big, but I'm small. I realize this today, just a few minutes ago. How old are you, Ohme? Thirty-five? Thirty-six?"

"I'm thirty-six."

"When I was about your age, I met somebody. I thought she was truly a goddess on earth. I had to control myself whenever I was around her because she was a married woman. X had just run away from home, and I didn't really have nobody to talk to. I used to run into her coming and going and we would talk, nothing serious. I just liked talking to her. She made my day. One day, we were talking, and this beautiful creature breaks down and starts crying and shit.

Seems her husband had just started doing drugs, and he was starting to kick her ass. I think she turned to me 'cause she was afraid and confused. I took her home, and one thing led to another. We regretted what happened and decided it would be best if we didn't see each other again, and I never told another soul until now. Her name was Mona, and, when I looked at that kid y'all brought in here today, I realized that Tee might be my kid."

I smile at Biggs because I know he can't just make that shit up. I tell him Tee's story and about the garbage room episode.

"Ohme, I need for you to keep this conversation a secret until I figure out what to do about X and Tee."

For the first time, since I've known Biggs, I realize that I could have taught him something: You don't fuck with married women, or your kid could end up in the garbage. Sorry, but it's true.

They announce that visiting hours are over, so it's time to go.

Biggs stands up and says, "I know you think this shit is funny. I know you. Just do what the fuck I said and don't say nothing."

"Alright! I got you. Call me later on."

Biggs nods at me and walks off.

On our way home, X wants to know what me and Biggs had talked about.

"We talked about business," I reply, but my smile drops a dime on me.

"Nah, for real. What did he say?" X asks. "I thought I heard him say he loved me."

"Yeah, he did say that."

I finally get X off my back. Luckily, it only takes a couple of days for me and X to find a building that will be perfect for our new restaurant. We take Tee and Ed with us to check it out.

CHAPTER FIFTEEN

THIS IS BUSINESS

ED

Tee comes upstairs and gets me.

"Come on, Ed. It's time to take care of business. X and Ohme are already in the car waiting.

We jump in the car X drives up to a rundown store front.

All I can say is "What the fuck?"

X starts talking, shit, "We can do this, and it's legit. There's no limit to the money we can make, and if you and Tee want in, you in; if not, get to steppin'."

Of course, I don't want in. This has to be some sort of a joke. I figure there has to be an angle, but I know, when it comes to making money, that X and Ohme have the game on smash. So, I think it would be best if I just play along.

"The restaurant is gonna be on the first floor, right?"

X is obviously serious about this shit.

"We gonna fix up the second floor and rent it out."

"We?" I ask. I can't take it no more. "We ain't construction workers. We hustlers."

"Nah, son. We business associates. This is a business."

Ohme always has to come with some bullshit. I can't say what I want to say, but, because I'm a grown-ass man, I know I have to say something.

"Hey! Look, X. I ain't trying to knock your hustle, but there's too much money out in these streets to just let it go. I hustle, that's what I do. That's all I know how to do. I can't stop."

Please let somebody else up in this car feel what I'm saying, I thinking.

"G.T., what you think?" I ask.

I know deep inside that G.T. feels the same way I do. That's my dawg.

"Well, G. What's up?" I ask again.

"Yo, Ed. I really don't think we got a choice. Ohme got the connect, while X got the workers and the customers. Let's just give this restaurant shit a try. If it works, cool. If not, to tell you the truth, I don't know what I'm gonna do."

I just look at this motherfucker. I can't believe it. They really going to flip burgers and serve cocktails and shit? X continues to talk about the restaurant, acting like what I said didn't mean jack.

The next morning, these fools get up early to go to work. That night, I came up with my own plan to get that dough. If I work with them for a couple of weeks, I figured that would give me enough time to find my own connect. These fools were up early the next morning, ready to go to work. I was bored as hell the first couple of hours. They ain't do shit but argue and write shit down in a book.

"We can put the bar here…The kitchen should be over there… Let's put a dance floor back there."

Back and forth, back and forth, like a married couple or something. G.T. ain't saying shit, and neither am I. I just want my money at the end of the day, and the day is going pretty good until we go upstairs.

Above the restaurant are three of the most busted apartments I have ever seen. To make matters worse, my sneakers get dirty, and I haven't even done any work. Day one is over and I wasted my time. I made sixty dollars. I guess because we didn't do nothing but walk around. I can't wait to get home and drink me some liquor, and, when I get home, that's what I do. I drink and pass right out. I feel like I only slept for twenty minutes when it's time to do it again. Up early in the morning and back to the dirty restaurant. Monday through Sunday. Sometimes ten, twelve hours a day. This shit is harder than hustling and for half the money.

Every day, I'm cutting something or hurting something. If it's not my back hurting, it's my feet hurting. My poor feet, get beat up and stink from sweating so much. I don't know how much longer I'm gonna be able to take this shit. The slave work is hard enough, but what makes it all unbearable is what happens when we got home. All I try to do is relax and have a good time, but all they want to do is talk about the restaurant. Who does that? Work all day and then come home to talk about work. After a few months of back-breaking work, ruining all my clothes and sneakers, having no fun at all, the restaurant is looking pretty good, I must admit. Not bad, not bad at all. True, there are no tables or chairs. We still don't have a kitchen or bar, and I still can't picture the dance floor, but, all in all, it's clean and the repairs. All I can think about is finishing and never coming back.

Finding a legit connect is harder than I thought. Everybody wants to try and get over on me because I'm a young dude. They don't know I have more business smarts in me than the average motherfucker. Another problem I'm having is with the old 4B crew. Well, what's left of them anyway. For every dollar that is made, Des got a cut. It seems like nobody has the heart to put him out of business. Well, got the heart; all I need is the patience. All my patience pays off one day. X and Tee are carrying tables and chairs into the restaurant, while me and Ohme are busy carrying Sheetrock up the stairs to the apartments. It's Ohme's fault. The heavy-ass drywall slips out of his hand and knocks me down the stairs. Even though I'm not paralyzed, I act like I am. Slavery is officially over, and I never go back to work in that motherfucker again. I now have all the time I need to find a connect and build up a clientele. At the same time, X and Ohme can't say shit about me being home all day. If I was in a union, I could sue their asses.

CHAPTER SIXTEEN

I GOT YOU SOMETHING, TOO

TEE

By the time my sixteenth birthday rolled around, we were just about finished with the restaurant, This was the hardest shit I had ever done in my life, but we did it. As an extra birthday present, I got the day off.

I was awakened by Ed's voice,, "Wake up, shorty! It's your birthday!"

"Wake me up later," I moan as I pull the covers up over my head.

"Come on, G.T.! Get up! X and Ohme left you some birthday presents in the living room."

After hearing that, I pulled the cover off my face and sit up in the bed.

"I got you something, too," he tells me as he picks up a book bag from off the floor. He sits on the edge of my bed and unzips the bag.

"I've been hitting the streets hard, while y'all motherfuckers been bullshitting. Soon, we gonna have enough money to get out of here."

Ed's face is glowing brighter than the green bricks of money in his book bag. I'm not impressed. If anything, I'm confused. I'm not impressed by the money, and I'm damn sure confused by his statement.

"Ed, what the fuck are you talking about?"

"I'm talking about me and you becoming us. Let's go get that villa suite like we talked about. Be my girl, G.T."

Confusion hits the roof. No! Confusion has just left the planet. My eyes explode open like popcorn.

"But...but we ain't like that! We like brother and sister, Ed. We like best friends, remember?"

As he inhales my words, his face stops glowing. His eyes must have taken the blood out of his face because his eyes turn red. His demeanor remains cool as he calmly says, "Yeah, we best friends, but what I feel for you is more than that."

He leans in closer to kiss me. I put my hands in front of my body to distance myself from him. At the same time, I lean back further and further on the bed to distance myself even more. He ends up on top of me while my hands end up buried beneath his body. Our lips meet like two planets colliding—subtle, at first; then, they explode.

"What the fuck are you doing?" I scream out.

I free my hands and connect numerous punches to his face. First, he grabs my right wrist and then my left. He holds them together with one hand, and, with his other hand, he pulled out his rock hard penis. Ed pulls my panties to the side and forced his way into my tight, dry hole.

"Stop, Ed! Please stop! Don't do this to me!"

The more pain I reveal, the more excited he becomes. I give up on trying to persuade him to stop and focus my energy on trying to free my hands. I toss, turn, twist, and kick. I squeeze my eyes tight to fight the pain. I hope that, when I open my eyes again, I will find it was all a nightmare. This has to be a dream. When I do open my eyes, I look up at the boy that used to be Ed. He looks like Ed, but Ed is gone. Just then, I remember something Ohme had once told me: "Don't ever let nobody take anything from you."

I can hear him saying it to me almost as if he is here in the room with me. I wish he was in here, so he could kill this bitch.

"You better stop before I tell Ohme and X," I half scream at him.

But Ed doesn't stop until his climax. It lasts two or three minutes tops, but it seems like two or three lifetimes to me. He pulls himself up off of me, triumphant and proud. He leans in to give me a kiss, but I turn my face to hide the tears. He tries to get me to turn around while he says, "I love you so much. I'm gonna make this dough and get us that villa suite. We ain't gonna have to worry about nothing."

When he realizes that I won't or can't face him, the fear of what is going to happen to him must have finally kicked in.

"G.T., let me tell you something. If you tell X and Ohme what happened they might fuck me up, but I will kill both of them. I've killed before, and I'll kill again, especially for you."

I lie on my bed and ignore everything he says. *I'm still telling on your ass*, I think to myself.

"Them motherfuckers gone soft, G.T. They washed up. We went from making hundreds of dollars a day to a couple hundred a week. What the fuck is that? I run this block now, so tell me, which one of them should I kill first? Huh, which one?"

Ed closes the book bag and slides it under his bed.

"It's your birthday, shorty. Go open your presents. I bought you a cake, too. It's in the refrigerator."

And just like that, he's gone.

I don't move for a long time. I just stay curled up in the bed. I cry quietly as I think about what had just been taken from me. I always thought my first time would be with the man of my dreams. Not with a backstabbing psycho bitch like Ed. It wasn't suppose to be like this.

Later that night, I hear somebody opening the front door of our apartment. I pray to God it isn't Ed. I don't have the courage to unlock the bedroom door to see who it is.

Knock! Knock! Knock!

"Tee, you in there? It's me. Ohme."

"Yeah, I'm in here, Ohme. What's up?"

"You had a good birthday?"

I pause, giving myself a minute to think before I answer. I want to run to the door and tell Ohme what Ed had done to me, but Ed had made a good point about X and Ohme being washed up. If it's true about Ed running the block now, X and Ohme would be the ones to get killed, not Ed.

"Yeah, it was alright, Ohme."

"You sure? 'Cause it don't sound like it was alright."

"Out of all days, my period had to come on my birthday. These cramps are kicking my ass."

"That's fucked up. Ya need anything?"

"Nah, I'm good," I manage to lie to him as I choke back the tears that have built up inside of me.

"That shit must be fucking you up, girl. You haven't even opened up your presents. I hope you feel better."

"Thanks Ohme."

"You seen Ed?"

I think about what Ed said again.

"Nah, I haven't seen him all day."

"Alright. Just stay away from me with that period shit. I'm sure you'll feel better tomorrow."

I give him a fake laugh, but tomorrow wasn't better nor the next day or the day after that. Even after many days had passed, I didn't feel better. In fact, I never went back to work at the restaurant. I told X and Ohme I was sick, and I was. In reality, I was pregnant. It took a couple of weeks before X and Ohme noticed the change in my appearance and personality.

One Friday, X comes into my room and sits down next to me on the bed.

"Your face is looking different, shorty. You pregnant or something?"

I stared at the wall and think hard before answering. This is the moment that will determine if one, two, three, four or, possibly, five people in 3B will live or die.

"I don't know, X. I mean, I think I am."

"Yo, Ohme! I told you she was pregnant!" X yells.

I hear Ohme jump up off the couch and fly past the small bootleg TV that sat inside the huge entertainment center.

"She's what?"

I raise my head to see Ohme standing at my bedroom door. He looks afraid to come close to the being that sits in my stomach.

"Whose is it? That little motherfucker Ed?"

Ohme's tone scares me, because he sounds like he's mad. I drop a couple of tears but hold back a million more as I tell him, "Yeah."

"My shit is packed, and I'm outta here."

I suck my teeth, "Come on, Ohme. Stop playing."

"Nah, for real, Tee. We out. The restaurant's finished. The upstairs apartments are finished, and we ready to go. We ready to open for business."

"Yeah," X chimes in. "We wanted you to come, too, but that was before we found out about you and Ed."

"It ain't nothing like that," I quickly respond. "Why you'll fucking with me?"

"So, if it ain't like that, then you coming with us?" X questions.

"I want to but—"

Before I can finish, we hear the front door open.

I'm so nervous and scared that everybody's about to get shot up in a hail of bullets.

"What's up? What's up?" Ed says as he squeezes past Ohme to enter the bedroom.

"Yeah! I heard about what you did," X looks at Ed accusingly..

Ed stops dead in his tracks. He looks at me, as he reaches into his coat pocket. I'm not sure what to make of his facial expression. It's cool, but it shows nervousness, too. Right then, I choose not to risk it.

"X and Ohme are moving out. We gotta pay the bills now."

Ed flashes me an edgy smile.

"Okay, Tee. What you going to do?" Ohme turns to me, purposely ignoring Ed. "You coming with us, or you staying here? Don't forget. It's not about you. It's about that little baby."

"Ba..ba..Baby? Who's pregnant?" Ed asks with a stupid look on his face.

"You know who's pregnant, motherfucker," X replies, "and you better take care of it, too."

The look of nervousness on Ed's face disappears as he finally understands..

"Yo, G.T.! I know you gonna let me take care of my baby. You have to stay here with me and my seed."

I have to stay here? I think to myself, *Nah, fuck this. I'm leaving with X and Ohme*, and, just as I am about to announce my decision, Ed makes an announcement of his own.

"Hey! Is it alright if I tell my boys to come in? They waiting for me on the staircase."

"This is your crib now," says Ohme. "You can do whatever you want."

Ed hauls ass out of the bedroom and apartment to go and get his boys.

"I'm asking you for the last time. You staying or you coming?"

If there was ever a time to say something, this would be the time. Ed would be coming back with his boys at any minute.

"Nah, X. I think I'm going to stay."

"Alright," Ohme draws in a long breath. "I'm going to drop off the rest of your money tomorrow. With that baby coming, you're going to need every last penny."

"Hey, Ohme! Can you hold it for me just a little bit longer... until I figure out my life?"

"Okay, but, if you need it, come down to the restaurant anytime."

Ohme kisses me on my cheek, and X gets up and does the same. Then, they both exit my room.

"Love ya, Tee," Ohme gives me half a smile. "Don't worry. Watch what God does next."

"Love you shorty,"X chimes in before they both disappear out my room...

"I love y'all, too," I whisper as I started to cry again. For the first time in a real long time, I am by myself.

CHAPTER SEVENTEEN

GHETTO FOR REAL

TEE

It wasn't long before I was working for Ed. I had his old job of dropping off book bags. Except, unlike before, I was taking book bags to neighborhoods that looked worse than mine, and, unlike before, I was doing it with a baby growing inside of me. Ed told me, "The cops would never fuck with a pregnant girl." In some ways, I guess he was right.

One morning, he tells me I have two book bags to drop off. I've been to the first drop off spot before. It's only a few blocks over. The second spot, I've never heard of, so I get the directions from Ed. *This one might be a little harder to find,* I think I will save this one for last. I take the first book bag to Apartment 5A. The apartment is always dirty and smelly and there's a caged pit bull in the living room, I'm always reluctant to go in.

"He don't bite," Macho always tells me, but I focus on the dog the whole time I'm there.

"Ed said to have his money by eight tomorrow night," I tell Macho as he takes the book bag and walks off.

It's like, after that moment, I no longer exist. Macho goes into his kitchen for his crack pipe, samples the product, and says the same thing every time.

"Yeah! It's a little light, but it's alright."

Right on cue. I walk the fuck out of there, away from the smell of burning rubber or the combustion of a soul. I head back home and grab the second book bag. I stop to change my sneakers because my feet are killing me, and I'm was glad that I had did t because the second spot is impossible to find. I walk from one end of Nostrand Avenue almost to the next end, trying to find the building. I do see a good-looking guy, dressed fresh and looking clean. He's standing in front of Building 2652, and I ask, "Excuse me. Can you tell me where to find 2502? I know I'm on the right street," I add confidently.

"I'm going to help you because I can see you got a bun in the oven," he says, grinning, showing the prettiest teeth I have ever seen. *Damn! He is fine*, I think to myself, as I stare into his dark brown eyes.

"You know, you really shouldn't be on your feet. You should be at home with your feet up, eating ice cream, while your man is rubbing your feet."

"Are you going to rub my feet for me?" I asked, flirticously

Everything he's saying to me is true. Plus, this guy is fly. I'm talking Tuff fly. If I wasn't pregnant, I would give him the pussy, still might.

"Hold up, homeboy. What's your name?" I finally remember to ask.

He gives me that smile again, "My friends call me Love."

"And why is that?"

"Because I would love to be friends."

We both had to laugh on that one.

"Okay, Love. Where's 2502? 'Cause my feet really do hurt."

"Alright, shorty, but, first, tell me your name."

"My name is Tee, but my friends call me Sparkles."

"And why is that?"

"Because I sparkle like the stars."

Once again, we find ourselves laughing at the bullshit we were give each other.

"I know where 2502 is, but wouldn't you like to grab some pizza first?" he ask, pointing at a pizza shop across the street.

I'm hungry; I'm tired, and he's cute. You better believe I'm getting me a slice.

So, there I am in a pizza shop, laughing and joking for the first time in a long time. In between two slices of pizza and a large fruit punch, I listen to Love as he tells me about himself.

"I'm not into the hustle and bustle. I have dreams of being a financial advisor one day."

I can dig it because, hopefully, I won't have to be out here hustling forever. I don't tell him that, though.

"I'm a college student looking for 2502. Sometimes, I tutor troubled kids."

Now, this guy is really interested in me. Me being pregnant doesn't seem to mean shit. It takes a real man to be with a woman that's already pregnant. If you ask me, I think he might be the one.

"I have to go to the bathroom," I tell him.

"Alright. I'm going to go ahead and pay for our food," he responds.

After we finish, we exit the pizza shop and start walking up the block.

"Sparkles, can I have your phone number?"

Damn! I should have known he would want to call me. I figure, *Okay, Tee. You like this guy, so why not just be straight up with him?*

"I can't, Love. My situation is kind of complicated, but you can give me yours if you like."

"You have a pen?"

I check my pockets, all the while knowing I don't..

"Maybe, there's one in your book bag," Love suggest.

"I doubt that. I mean, I left all my pens on the kitchen table at home. That's where I do my intellectual work."

"Wait a minute. I might have one."

Love unzips his jacket and goes into his inside pocket.

"Okay, Sparkles. Do you know what this is?"

He flashed a shiny object at me, and I blink twice before I realize it's a gun.

"I have some free financial advice for you. I advise you to give me the book bag."

I'm not really scared. Yeah, I'm scared of the gun, but I'm not scared of the guy. His demeanor isn't threatening, and I can't really tell if he's for real.

"I'm not a mean guy, Sparkles. I've got friends who would shoot a man, women, or child, even a pregnant chick, if they hesitated about giving it up."

I've heard enough, so I reach out to put the bag in his hand before he can say another word.

"Thank you," he says smoothly. "I had a wonderful lunch, but you really shouldn't be out here hustling."

Love almost makes me feel like he's doing me a favor. I'm left standing here, feeling seduced, as well as stupid. I quickly decide to get the hell out of here before Love comes back and takes everything I own. I got three blocks up, and I see a police car. I run into the street and flag them down.

"Excuse me," I manage to say while huffing and puffing from the short jog to the car. "I just got robbed for my book bag!"

The two cops look at each other. Then, one says, "Well, I wonder what she had in the book bag?"

He never even looks my way.

"Oh...I...it was nothing but my books," I stutter.

When the light turns green, they drive away. That's why I hate the fucking police.

I never find 2502, but I do find the train station. I take a train that drops me off close to X and Ohme's restaurant. On my way there, I passed by a cleaners, and I saw my refection in the store window. *Man! Look at me, what have I become?* I can't answer because I don't know.

I kept on walking past a few more stores but stop when I see a huge butterfly light and under it a sign that reads BUTTERFLY RESTAURANT and LOUNGE. The animated butterfly was actually neon lights that seems to actually flutter. It's beautiful, and I find myself smiling as I go inside.

I'm stopped by a girl who is a little bit older than me. She ask, "Do you have a reservation, or is this your first time to Butterfly's?"

I see my reflection in the mirror hanging on the wall behind her. *A wreck.* I, suddenly, realized what I had become. *A wreck.* I look at her standing there, grinning at me, and brushing a few strands of hair that seem to have escaped her freshly done hair. With hands that definitely are manicured, she brushes invisible lint from her outfit.

"My first time? I helped build this shit, bitch! Where the hell is X and Ohme?"

"Bitch? Who you calling bitch, bitch?"

We go back and forth until Ohme comes up front.

"Tee! Tee! Calm down, baby! Michelle's just doing her job."

Ohme takes me by the arm and leads me to the back. I'm amazed at how incredible the restaurant looks.

"Hey, Ohme! It looks dope in here, but where's X?"

Ohme shook his head and said, "X got into a little altercation."

He passes me a glass of ice tea and ask, "Tee, are you hungry?"

"No, I'm not hungry. What happened to X?"

I forget about my crazy day for a minute.

"Let's just say that X's got bad people skills, always pulling out guns on the customers."

Ohme laughs, but I think it's serious until he eases my worries.

"Biggs told me to let the idiot rot for a couple of days. I'm going to post bail tomorrow."

Ohme's facial expression changes, "Enough about that. Is there anything you want to tell me 'cause I've been hearing some things in the street?"

"Like what?"

"That's what I'm asking you, Tee." Ohme is now all serious and shit.

I tell him everything about my hustling for Ed and about getting robbed, but I leave out the part about my rape. Ohme gives me a look that says he wants more from me, but, then, he just shrugs it off.

"Tee, I almost forgot."

He comes from behind the bar and walks out the door. He's gone for a few minutes, and, when he returns, he's carrying a plastic bag. I'm thinking he packed me some dinner because I can see the outline of food containers in the bag.

"I don't want you in 3B with a lot of money, but I'm giving you half your dough."

He ties a knot in the top of the plastic bag and handed it to me like it was number five on the dinner menu.

"Where's your chain?" he ask. "Don't tell me that got ripped off, too."

"Hell no!" I tell him. "I tuck that sucker in my shirt and zip up my jacket every time I leave the house."

"Alright. Hand it over, and no, I'm not robbing you."

I take off the chain and pass it to him. He slides a gold colored key onto the chain and passes it right back to me.

"Tee, listen up close to every word I'm about to say. This is the most important thing I've ever told you."

I position myself to catch every word Ohme is about to say.

"The world is yours, baby girl, but don't let that building become your whole world."

Ohme stops talking for a minute, like he's searching for the right way to say what comes next.

"You got to rise above that 3B and 4B bullshit. You got to take it up a level, shorty."

I ask Ohme, "What do you mean?"

But he still wouldn't give me a straight answer.

"Rise above 3B and 4B and don't never look down. Now, come on. I'm gonna drive your ass home."

When I get back to my house, I tell Ed what happened, and he seems more concerned about the book bag than me. I give him some money to replace the work that I had lost and tell him straight up, "My hustling days are over! I quit!"

After that, Ed starts to come up in the game fast, but my stomach is coming up faster.

CHAPTER EIGHTEEN

UNBELIEVEABLE PAIN

TEE

When my water breaks, I'm all alone, like always. Ed is out somewhere hustling. X and Ohme are all I had left, and they're gone. There's no pain, just a sudden gush, like I've pissed on myself. *No need to panic. I got this,. And calling an ambulance is out of the question. I'm not eighteen, and I don't have a mother or a father. Who knows? They might try to put me in a foster home. I've got to do it alone or, at least, get started until Ed comes home.*

Once the pain kicks in, I wish I had gone to the hospital or clinic or something. It's like somebody is stomping on my stomach and pussy at the same time. There is no time. The baby is coming.

Okay! I gotta calm down, I tell myself. I take big breaths. Then, I blow them out. Holding my stomach, I waddle from the living room to the bedroom, from the bedroom to the kitchen, and then back into the living room. Finally, I turn around and make my way to the hallway closet. I pull out as many towels as I can carry and make my way to the bathroom.

All those trips to the library, all the books I had read were finally going to pay off. I had read a book about a lady giving birth in the Mississippi River back in the slavery days. I drop the towels in the bathtub to make it comfortable, like a bird's nest.

Oh, shit! I need more towels! When I turn back around to walk out the bathroom, a pain rips through me. It it's like nothing I have ever felt before. I hold on to the wall, paralyzed, until the pain lest up enough for me to make my move. I creep my way to the closet and pull down sheets, towels, pillow cases, everything that is within my reach. Once I get back into the bathroom, I drop the extra stuff in the bathtub. I keep a few towels on the side for when the baby arrives. I raise my leg to climb into the tub, but, at the last minute, I remember that I forgot something. I put my foot back on the floor and reach into the medicine cabinet. I grab the alcohol and scissors and placed them close to the tub. I fill the bathtub up with a little bit of warm water. I let my bathrobe drop off my swollen body and slowly drop my wet panties. I climb into the tub just in time to brace myself for the next contraction. My screaming should have awaken the dead. With no other place to put my feet, I put one foot up against the soap dish while my other leg dangled outside of the tub.

I can't see the bloody liquid seeping out of me, but I can see the water changing colors. When the next contraction hits, I'm ready. I push and scream at the same time. Still, I can't see in between my legs, but I know the baby isn't out yet. I immediately start psyching myself out for the next contraction. *I can do this! I can do this! I don't need nobody! I can do this!* I take a deep breath in and blow it out. Then, another and another. My body is tired, but I give it my heart and soul. I know, if I don't, me and my baby are going to die in this bathtub. *Oh, God! Please don't let us die in this bathtub!* I brace for yet another contraction and coach myself.

"Alright, Tee! You can do this."

The contraction reaches its highest point when I hear a voice. It might be the voice in my head telling me, "Push, Tee! Push!"

In the library books, there was usually another person coaching the pregnant woman on.

Why I don't have nobody? I ask myself. *Why am I alone with this voice in my head that sounds like me?* When the pain hits again, the voice tells me to push with all my might, I give it all I have and then some. This time, there is no scream because I have no more energy to scream. Pop. The muscles in my pussy give way and the baby slides out and into the discolored water. I quickly snatch the baby out the water and take a deep breath. He was moving, so I exhale. I don't want to do it, but it has to be done. I grab the scissors off the floor and cut the umbilical cord. I lean over the side of the bathtub and gently placed my son on the towels that lay on the floor. I pour some alcohol on a hand towel and lay it across where I had just cut the umbilical cord. Perfect timing too, another contraction hits me, and I find myself pushing again, without even having to tell myself to push. Out comes another baby. At least, at first, I think it's a baby. When I take a closer look, it looks more like a balloon with all kinds of shit around it. There's a nasty liquid inside. I don't know what the fuck it is. All I know is that I don't want to touch it. It is then that I remember reading about the afterbirth in one of my books, and that is when it dawns on me. My real baby hasn't cried yet. I scoop him up and pop him gently on his ass, and that is when it happens. He lets out a cry like a cat that has just had his tail stepped on. Crying and laughing myself, I place him back down on his makeshift bed and climbed out of the tub.

CHAPTER NINETEEN

THE BEST THING TO EVER HAPPEN TO ME

ED

As soon as I walk through the door, I can tell something is wrong. There is a trail of funny looking stains going from the living room to the hallway and then from the hallway to the bathroom and from...

"Yo! G.T.! G.T.!" I yell out again and again as I follow the stains on the carpet. With the nozzle of my heater, I slowly push open the bedroom door. I can see G.T., lying on the bed. She has her back to me. She looks still enough to be dead.

I make my way around the bed, so I could see her face. In her arms, she's holding a towel, but I still can't tell if she is breathing or not. I put my heat away and move in closer. I'm shocked as I stare at the two of them. G.T. opens her eyes and looks up at me.

"Come on. I'm taking y'all to the hospital."

"I'm not going to no hospital," she whispers. "They might take my baby away. Just take your son for a bit, so I can get some sleep."

Hearing those words was like somebody telling me to take a million dollars.

"Be real careful," she tells me, but she doesn't have to worry. I carefully reach down and take my son from her. I carry him into X's old room and lay him down on the bed.

"I'm gonna call you Lil Ed after your daddy."

*****

G.T. is looking a lot better. I was worried she wasn't going to make it for the first couple of days. When I came home and seen she'd delivered the baby by herself, I had to go out and get this crack head nurse to check on her and Lil Ed. I had to make sure they was alright. I gave the nurse free drugs when she brought me supplies from the hospital. I could tell G.T. appreciated it because she didn't have that "I hate you" look on her face.

Lil Ed was the best thing that ever happened to me. Every time I looked at his face, I saw a little bit of me and a little bit of G.T. He had tan skin that glowed, compared to my white skin and G.T.'s chocolate complexion.

One Monday, I'm in the kitchen, cooking dinner. I've been doing that a lot lately, not hustling as much as I used to or should be. I can't complain, though. I figure I can help out at home and try to make up for what I had done to her.

G.T. is in the bathroom, giving little Ed a bath, so I yell, "Hey, G.T.! Dinner's ready!"

She doesn't answer me. It could be because the bathroom door is closed or she might've been ignoring me. That is probably the real reason.

Knock! Knock! Knock! Neither one of us can ignore that hard knock at the front door.

"Who the fuck is it?" I yell out as I unlock the front door.

Boom! Des kicks open the front door as I open it. It knocks me backwards and down to the floor. He puts his gun to my head.

"I'm not fucking playing with you, and I'm only going to ask you one time. Where's the drugs and the money at?"

I'm a little scared, but I keep my cool. My ego won't let a single word come out my mouth. He looks me in my eyes but doesn't see what he was looking for. He shoots once, striking me in the middle of my forehead. I can feel my lower body twitching, but I can't stop it. I have to...

CHAPTER TWENTY

JUST STARTINTG TO FORGIVE YOU

TEE

I recognize Des's voice as I stand frozen behind the bathroom door. The gunshot confirms what I already know about Des. He's a cold-blooded motherfucker who could kill without thinking twice about it. I locked the door, cut off the light, and back up slowly while holding Lil Ed tightly in my arms. The bathroom seems to shrink once I realize I can't back up no more. The back of my legs hit the edge of the tub, knocking me backwards and into the bath tub. My head flies back, hitting the tile wall hard as I land on my ass. I hold Lil Ed even tighter, from the time my feet leave the floor to the time I pull my legs into the tub. My body is sideways, curled up in the fetal position. *At any minute, Des is going to kick down this door and kill me and my baby. Did he hear me fall into this tub?* I wonder. *Nah, he didn't hear me.*

*****

DES

I did hear something. I cautiously approach the bathroom door with my gun aimed straight ahead. I'm not sure who is in there. *Is the person or persons behind the bathroom door holding heat?* I squeeze off four shots. Then, I quickly step to the side, pressing my back as hard as I can to the wall. When nobody shoots back at me or moans, I immediately go into the bedroom to get what I came for. I go straight for the beds and flip them upside down. First, G.T.'s bed; then, Ed's.

"There you are."

Under Ed's bed, I find the two book bags full of money, but I'm not finished yet. I fling open the closet door and toss their shit all over the bedroom floor, so I can find the rest of what I came for. The drugs are in the gym bag, just like we had thought they would be. As I make my way out the bedroom, I stop and look back at the room I had just destroyed. With all the excitement, I don't notice the Pampers, the tiny clothes, or the other baby items that are spread out around the room. I turn my attention to the bathroom door again. I stare at it, trying to decide whether to kick it in or not. I remember the plan and slowly walked past the bathroom door. I look back at it once or twice. This isn't how I usually handle my business. I make sure to slam the door after leaving the apartment.

*****

TEE

I lay in the bathtub, still holding on to Lil Ed. I am too scared to cry; afraid even my tears will make a noise. The bullets that had flown through the bathroom door paralyzed me. Fortunately, it's all in my mind. Neither me or my baby have been hit by the flying bullets as they ricocheted off the walls and porcelain in the bathroom.

I hear Des as he ransacks the bedroom. Then, I hear the front door slam. *It's a trick to get me out of the bathroom,* I figure. Lil Ed begins to cry. I put my hand over his mouth. I'm not sure what I am going to do next, until I remember what X had told me about Des and Blackbaby. If he can love a dog, then maybe he can have compassion for Lil Ed. I'm as good as dead because he hates my guts, but Lil Ed still has a chance.

I climb out the bathtub, holding on tightly to Lil Ed, and I slowly walk to the bathroom door. I put my ear against it and try to hear, but nothing is going on as far as I can tell. I open the door and stick my head out. Luckily, there is no one in the apartment as far as I can see, but what I do see is Ed's feet sticking out from behind the wall. I walk closer, and I can see his legs, and, even closer is his waist. I got as close as I am willing to get, because I can see Ed's face has a hole in it. The blood and brain fragments were scattered on the floor and wall.

I look down at Ed and all I can do is shake my head in disbelief. *Damn, Ed! We used to be friends. Yeah, I hate your guts for what you did to me, but I was just starting to forgive you. I feel sorry for you. We have a kid together…*So many things race through my mind, and that is when the fear sets back in. *What if Des comes back? He's going to kill me and my baby.* I step over Ed's body and walk out the front door.

CHAPTER TWENTY-ONE

RISE ABOVE IT

TEE

I don't know where I'm going or what I'm going to do when

I get there. Once in the hallway, the garbage room seems to be the safest place to go. My mind is racing. *What if Des is downstairs or in front of the building?* I run to the garbage room, still holding Lil Ed close to me. I open the door, step inside, and take my usual seat on top of some trash bags. Only this time, it's not just my life I'm trying to save. I'm back in the garbage room tomb with Lil Ed. Last time, it was on the fourth floor; this time, it's on the third. Like the room above, this room is dark, and, once again, the light shines through from the bottom of the door. Once again, the rotten smells fills my nose, and I know the nasty creatures are keeping me company again. I close my eyes, even though it is already dark. I then do something I have never done before— I talk to God. I do not pray to God; I talk to God.

"I really don't know you like I should. I mean, I don't know who you are, not really. I don't know if you're X's Christian God, or if you're Ohme's Muslim God. You might even be Ed's parents' Jehovah. I really don't know, but, if you look in my heart, you'll see I'm not a bad person. Why do I keep ending up in here? Can you please help me? Please! I promise that I'll change. Just tell me what you want me to do."

Tears roll down my face and onto the towel that Little Ed is wrapped in. I sit motionless, like a statue waiting for God to respond. I'm hoping God will send somebody to help me, but no one ever came. I hope God will speak to me, but no one says a word.

My mind slips away to that place where sanity went when it can't take no more. I absentmindedly click the butterfly medallion together with the gold colored key that hangs around my neck. Lil Ed is so quiet. He must be asleep. I close my eyes, and I am no longer in the garbage room. I can't explain where I am. I can only try to explain what I feel. There is no universal word for what it. All I can say is that I feel the most powerful, humbling feeling I've ever felt in my life. And it can only come from whatever loves me, you, and us the most. The only true love there is, who would like to remain nameless, and whose face would like to do the same, the one whom self-made gods and humans owe their existence to. Neither space nor time can keep up. Most minds can't grasp what I see in this garbage room. The same way we can't grasp what we see in themselves. How many mornings have I woken up, opened my eyes, and I still couldn't see? How long had I walked around blind? How long was I asleep? How long was I dead? Even now, I'm falling asleep as Lil Ed moves in my arms. I can't stay here forever in this heaven. I just woke up to tell you God loves you. The name *God* is an understatement, and the word *love* is an understatement, too. Much, much, much you have to see for yourself. This is coming from one being to another.

I open my eyes, and it's still dark in the garbage room.

"Don't worry boo-bee. We going to be alright."

Lil Ed hears my voice and starts crying. Sometimes, you can say something, and you only make it worse. I look down to see if I can see his face. If I can only catch a glimpse of him or him a glimpse of me, it might be enough to get him to stop crying. There is too much darkness in the room, and I couldn't...

Wait! Wait a minute! The light from under the door was hitting the diamonds in my butterfly medallion just right. It lets off a small shine that seems to give life to the room. I think about my moms and my pops and X and Ohme and Tuff. And, now, Ed is dead, too.

I think about everything X and Ohme have taught me. The last time I had seen Ohme, he'd told me to rise above the garbage room tomb bullshit, all the 3B and 4B bullshit.

"Take it to the next level. Rise above it."

The gold colored key Ohme had placed on the chain was reflecting off the medallion.

Oh, my God! I immediately stand up and open the garbage room door. The lights are bright, only because I had been in the dark for so long. I waited a few seconds for my eyes to finally adjust. When everything is clear, I run to the stairs with Lil Ed wrapped safely in my arms. I open the door and run up to the fourth floor, but I don't stop there. I keep on running until I get to the fifth floor. I fling open the staircase door and run directly to Apartment 5B. I have risen above the bullshit in 3B and 4B. I pull my chain up over my head. Then, I try to connect the key with the hole. It takes me four or five tries before I finally turned the key in the lock, and, with shaking hands, I turn the doorknob. If Des was chasing me, I would be dead.

I open the door slowly, not knowing what to expect, but I'm surprised to see nothing in the apartment. Nothing at all, except a table in the living room. It sort of reminded me of the old crib me and Moms used to have. There is a long brown envelope on the table. *Could it be? After all this time, is she still alive?* I gently lay Lil Ed on the table and open the envelope.

*****

X

Oh, man! I hope you get this letter. If anything happened to you or your baby, Des already knows what's going to happen to him. My pops said you were smart, so, if you took that key and made it to 5B, you're more than smart; you're blessed. If you haven't figured it out already, I had to do this. Ohme and Des ain't never get along, but they sat down for hours planning Ed's future. I know about everything that went down. I know he raped you on your birthday — that bitch— and I know you've been hustling with him. The streets is always watching. I should have did a better job of watching you. I told Mona she couldn't take care of you and look at the job I did. I did a worse job than she did. I'm so sorry, Tee.

Shorty, I ain't never tell nobody this before. Well, maybe my pops and Ohme, but, yo, Tee, I really love you, and you changed my life. I didn't save you from the garbage room; you saved me. Look in the fridge when you done reading this. There's one more book bag in there for you. I threw in a bus ticket that's gonna take you back to the villa. You got two hundred and fifty thousand dollars, a baby, and a new start. Don't fuck it up. Ohme's letter is next. Maybe, we'll come out there and see you one day. Give that baby a kiss for me, he most important part you can play now is to be a mother to your child.

Peace. Love ya.

TEE

I'm confused about everything that has happened in the last year. *How could they have found out about what Ed did to me? How did they know I was hustling with him?* I'm anxious to read what Ohme has to say. I put X's letter down and began to read Ohme's.

*****

OHME

What's up, Tee? What's up? What's down? What's inside of you and outside of you? You already know. I sealed this envelope up myself. I can't let X know what I'm about to tell you. Remember that day we went to go visit Biggs at the prison? Well, to give it to you raw, you might be Bigg's daughter. I know you loved your pops, but I gotta keep it real with you. Biggs and your mom's had a little something going on back in the days. Don't get upset, baby. We all share the same ancestors back in Africa anyway. I don't know if I can hold this secret from X forever. I think Biggs is testing my manhood again. Why else would he tell me to keep a secret like this from my best friend, my partner in crime, my wifey? Oh, you didn't know? Me and X used to be married. With all the fighting and arguing, plus the fact that we weren't able to have kids, it wasn't too long before we drifted apart. That was until she found you. She told me that very same night, "Ohme, I look in that little girl's eyes, and I seen myself. I prayed to the father of Jesus himself, and I asked him to make a way. I asked if he could fix all of this shit." I agreed with her and started asking Allah for the same thing. The God that loves us most will sure nuff make a way. God will make a way. I sure do wish my boy Tuff could see us now. Speaking of Tuff, did you know? Probably not. We came to check on you one day. We tried to check on you every day, and, late one night, we went to 4B, and, surprisingly, no one was there except for Des. He tells us he has something to show us and leads us to one of the back rooms. You'll never guess what I saw. Your TV that got robbed out of 3B. The one that was in your and Ed's room. He said he would still be watching that shit, too, if he didn't get up one day and see your "bitch-ass name written on the side of it". Those were his words, not mine. He said Bam and Shy had brought your TV into 4B a long time ago. X asked him where Bam and Shy was at now, and he told us to hold on. I thought this prick was getting a beer because I heard the refrigerator door open and then close. He comes back with a smile on his face and places a bag on top of the TV. It sounded like frozen hamburger meat hitting the pan. He unwrapped the bag and told us to shake their hands. Des says it was Bam and Shy that robbed our crib. Bad move on their part because I always knew Des had a thing for X. Who knows what else *went on when I wasn't around? Before Shy and Bam had their unfortunate accident, Shy had told Des where something very important was hidden, behind a radiator. It was Ed's journal.*

I ripped out two pages from the journal. I thought you should read them for yourself. The stove works, so I want you to burn these letters before you go. I promised Biggs I would put something extra in the book bag for you, too.

Love always and always loving you,
Ohme

*****

TEE

I love that dude. Man, I loved them both, and, if Biggs really was my pops, then I guessed I can have love for him, too. I can't believe that, after all this time, I have a sister. A sister who had lived in the same building as me. We lived in the same house, and I didn't even know. I turn Ohme's letter over to see if there is anymore, but there's nothing on the back. What was he talking about? What does he think I should read? I open the long brown envelope and way at the bottom was a folded up piece of paper. I take it out only to discover there are two pieces of paper in it.

*****

ED

3/29/1990

Am I lucky or what? Not only did my future wife not die in the garbage room, but we moving into a new apartment together with X and Ohme. Fuck them! Watch me get the pussy, even if I gotta take it. I just got to be patient. Wait for the right time to make my move and then get that.

12/31/1992

Why am I on the staircase with Tuff, and this motherfucker tells me he had a pit bull back in the day. This famous pit bull he had just so happened to be the same pit that almost killed my shorty. He told me he felt bad about what happened to her and the little kid that day. He had the nerve to tell me, of all the people in the world, that he was the one responsible for what happened to my baby. I asked him why the fuck did he let the dog loose in the first place. He tells me some bullshit about it being his uncle's dog, and it never let the other dogs in the house eat. He tied the pit up in the staircase and forgot about it. He forgot about it? I got something for him and Des's punk ass, too. Boom! Bye. Bye.

*****

TEE

I want to read more, but there is no more. Now, I understand what Tuff was trying to tell me that day, coming home from the library. It's sad because I would have forgiven him if he would have only told me, instead of confiding in Ed. I don't even hate Ed for what he did to me that day. I have a beautiful son now, and I love life. One by one, I burn the pages to a crisp. I remove the book bag from the fridge. I've been running book bags for a long time, so I can tell by the weight of this one that there is more money in this one than I have ever felt before.

I throw the bag over my shoulder and pick Lil Ed up off the table. I walk out the apartment and head for the elevator. My heart is racing, beating so hard through my chest that it pushes Lil Ed up and down, like a boat caught in a hurricane. I want to take the stairs, but I second guessed myself and take the elevator.

It goes down so slow, but then stops on the fourth floor. I hold my breath as the elevator door opens. Before I know it, Des is in the elevator with me. My heart skips a beat, not once but twice. I lose my breath and almost drop Lil Ed. I put my head down and take a deep breath. Death is in the elevator with me. Lil Ed begins to cry hysterically.

"I didn't know you had a baby, G.T."

I don't respond because there is no need to. I knew I'm beat. I know when it's over. I wait for my life to flash before my eyes, but it doesn't. Something worse than that happens. Des holds out his hands.

"Pass me the baby, G.T."

I don't say a word. I put my bag of money on the floor, just as the elevator touches down in the lobby. The door slides open. I lay Lil Ed on the bag and bum rush Des. I push him up against the wall. He looks at me as if I've done something wrong to him. I can't turn back now. I scratch him in his face three or four times before he even knows what hit him. He is able to punch me in my nose; it shocks me more than it hurts me. I move in close to him, so he can't hit me again. All I want to do is keep him away from my baby. I fight him tooth and nail. I mean, I really bite down on his face. Instead of stopping him, this just makes him angrier. He tightly grabs my shirt and cocks back his hand for a knockout blow. I see it; I could almost feel it before it strikes. Everything goes from moving real fast to slow motion. As a final act of desperation and reflex, I knee him with all my might in his balls. The best way to describe his facial expression is a man with the worst stomach ache I have seen. The best way to describe the noise is I can literally hear his manhood leaving his body. I knee him again while his mouth is open, gasping for air. He looks like a broken branch in the elevator, folded up and all bent. I pick up Lil Ed and my bag. As I lay the bag on my shoulder, Des is right on the verge of standing up from his crouched position. Do you remember playing kickball in school? Well, this is what it looks like when my toes meet his teeth. I run out the elevator, but not before pushing the eighth and sixth floor buttons. I run out of the lobby and onto the city street.

Lil Ed is still crying hysterically. Can I blame him? He probably senses that we were just fighting for our lives. I knew God knows because a lady is stepping out of a cab, right in front of my building. She holds the car door open for me.

"Oh, my God! Are y'all okay?"

"We're fine, miss. Thank you so much."

I jump in that cab and yell, "Hurry up! Just drive! Drive!"

The driver pulls off, and I got to smile. I bounce Lil Ed in my arms as I try to calm him down.

"It's alright, boo-bee. It's alright now."

"Where to, lady?" the cab driver asks me, while passing me a load of napkins from the driver's side door and then more from the glove compartment. My nose is busted up and blood covers the bottom half of my face. I can taste the metallic flavor of blood now and still can't believe the shit that just happened.

"Greyhound bus station," I answer as our eyes met in the mirror. "I feel better than I look," I assure him.

As the cab picks up speed, I take one last look out the back window, afraid even now that

Des can still catch me. In my mind, I see him running after the cab, and, just as quickly, I see Ohme step out of nowhere and fuck Des up. I face the driver and my future and think to myself, *I'll take it any way that I can.*

EPILOGUE

TEE

When me and Lil Ed finally make it to the villa, I realize there is something special about today. I feel different. I have a feeling that, no matter what happens, in life, as well as death, shit is going to be alright.

I hide my dough in the bottom of the trash can, and then I put the trash bag back in the can. I give me and my little snuggle bear a bath, made a couple of bottles, and head outside to the phat parade I seen over on the boardwalk. I catch up to the festival right over there on Main Street. The breeze is nice and cool. It seems like there's thousands of people on the street, marching and dancing. They're smiling and laughing, and I see a couple of people smoking spliffs while Bob Marley's "Stir It Up" blast in the background. I have never seen a sight like that before. People happy, and getting along, but, even with all these people around me having a good time, even with Little Ed in my arms, I can't help suddenly feeling like I am very alone. I find a spot under a palm tree and continue to watch the many different faces celebrating. I know that everything happens for a reason, and, in life, there are no coincidences, and, as if to put a period on my final conclusion, a beautiful, colorful butterfly flies around my head and lands on my shoulder.

I'm not alone. Can you see it? Do you feel it? Can you love it?

The Beginning